LIONESS

LIONESS

By
Kristin Kennedy
MJ Politis

www.wickedpublishing.net
wickedpublishingllc@gmail.com

BOOK 1
LIONESS
KRISTIN KENNEDY
M.J. POLITIS
Wicked Publishing

Lioness

First Edition

Published through Wicked Publishing LLC 2017

Credits

Editor: Adrian J. Smith

Cover Design by Shiralyn Lee

ISBN-13:978-1542933360
ISBN-10:1542933366

Dedication

This book is dedicated to the victims of human trafficking and to all those who have no voice.

Acknowledgements

I would like to thank my parents instilling a fire that refuses be extinguished within me.

I would also like to thank Dawn Carter and Shiralyn Lee, my publishers at Wicked Publishing for believing in me, and turning my dream of being published into reality.

And thank you to my editor Adrian J Smith for taking on the task of editing Lioness and with a gentle hand, guiding myself and my co-author, MJ. Politis, making Lioness flawless.

Synopsis

Leona Zimmerman is one of the first transgender university research biologists in New England, whose innovative scientific work and Spiritual insights are well ahead of her time. Everything in her life was going as planned until her brother presumably committed suicide. When she returned home to lay her brother to rest, she soon discovered her brother's place of employment was actually a front for human trafficking, sex-slavery, and illegal arms sales. She knew then that there was more to her brother's death than what she was told. But what?

CHAPTER 1

A bright light penetrated Leona Zimmerman's tired eyes as she strolled into the large lecture hall. *It's time to get this bullshit started!*

With a wave of her hand, she choked the beam of light that emanated from the projector, causing it to cast a mixture of obscured shadows on the wall behind her—her tapered fingers emphasized by the magnification, appearing as if they could reach out and grab one of the silhouette figures quietly seated.

The overwhelming odor of male sweat mixed with floral and citrus notes from females generated disgust. She tried to take in quick shallow breaths, but the torturous smells made her nostrils flare and her stomach flip while she suffered in silence.

"This is Rover," she said, pointing to the illuminated image on the screen of a Labrador Retriever. "Get used to seeing him. He might be on one of your tests." The three hundred plus new students sat quietly in front of her, and most were showing an interest by looking at the screen.

With the click of a finger, the screen changed, and she looked at the illuminated words. The standard learning material, which had been co-authored by the department head and was mostly inaccurate. It made her stomach churn, but there was little she could say.

One of the students cleared their throat, bringing Leona back into real time. It was Rachel Garrison, the most independent mind in the room and perhaps the entire university. The long-haired auburn neo-hippie with the anti-anything establishment flicked her hand, discretely motioning for her professor to be responsible and move on with something other than silence.

Leona smiled, cursed under her breath, and then clicked on the PowerPoint for the day's lesson.

"Toxins, Antidotes, and Mechanisms of Action," she spoke with as much self-enforced lifelessness as possible, in the exact words and subtext of the officially-approved terminology.

Leona read the required material word for word and several times she had to inhale a frustrated breath when the material contradicted the truth. As if waking up from a trance, she did a sudden double take. Nothing she read was factual, in fact, she was teaching half-truths. She was no better than those she despised, and as much as she fought the injustice, she was still supporting medical fairytales.

"No matter what I teach you throughout this semester, I want you to challenge me."

The infusion of Leona's re-found bravado stopped dead in its tracks when she looked up at her reflection, a warrior princess in the glass above the last row of slumbering students. Next to that reflection, just beyond the discretely opened door, was John Ditka. More accurately, her boss and Chairman of the Biological Sciences Department. His lab coat neatly pressed, his eyes framed by wire-rimmed glasses, and every graying hair on his aristocratic head in perfect place.

With a slight movement of his fingers, he suggested Leona say what was on the pre-approved party-line overheads rather than what was on her mind. It was a last warning that Ditka meant this time.

Render unto Caesar that which is Caesar's, Leona recalled as something Jesus suggested to the wise and commanded to the ignorant as a way to not get screwed by the suits. *But give to God that which is God's,* she remembered as the rest of that credo, as well as that Jesus was crucified for living such words. Leona was okay with sacrificing herself for the Truth, but unlike Jesus, she had no "Dirty Dozen" of Jewish publicists to carry on her work. Rachel, her prodigy, was at best fledgling "disciple" material.

Ditka pointed again toward the screen. This time his suggestion from his hidden position in the hallway was a command. Leona flipped on to the next overhead and winced at the narrow-mindedness of the printed material with the lifeless graphics associated with it.

"The established protocols for antidote administration for commonly observed toxins are…" she read with eyes turned down, adopting as lifeless a voice as possible. She continued to pass on the data on the overhead word for word without any rhythm or musicality in her speech.

It seemed to please Ditka, as she'd been hired as a researcher rather than a teacher. She felt more like a messenger, passing on party line bullshit rather than encouraging critical, expansive thinking.

Leona had no choice but to play with the game at hand, pretending to be a dulled out professional scientist to soothe the undeveloped minds and slumbering spirits of the "what do we have to know for the exam" students. The act out was intended as a goof for those who could understand it was satire so they could have a much-needed private laugh, but the most important person in the room wasn't laughing—Rachel, her prodigy.

"I paid three-hundred dollars a credit from my own fucking pocket for this bullshit!" Rachel mouthed under her breath. "This revolutionary lecturer is betraying me, just like everyone else. Do you expect us to give up the revolution business like everyone else has? Do you want us to just go with the flow? Or throw our lives into the toilet?"

Leona looked away, as she was now committed to making nice with the devil, so she could steal his fire and use it against him in a heavenly cause. "The standard treatments for toxic exposure in dogs have been carefully and thoroughly worked out by the North American Veterinary Association," she continued, with a wide, made-for-the-photo-of-the-alumni-magazine smile.

She stopped, noting Ditka had left. Though that carrier of Dull Out Virus had departed, other demons came into her head. With her acute sense of hearing, she heard Rachel close her books and recalled her own past of hopelessness and blank stares.

"Do a little harm now to stop a lot of harm later," was the rationalization Leona's bosses had told her. "You're all privileged to be necessary evils for a greater good," was the battle used to justify so much of what she'd witnessed and done in the past.

"It's time for the truth." Grabbing the chalk with force, the bones in her fingers creaked. She loaded the blackboard behind the overhead with her own work and others whose work would never be published as long as Professor Doctor Ditka's sat on the editorial board of the journals.

"And as for other toxins that have killed a lot more animals and people than the ones in this textbook," she continued by describing the mechanisms of action and potential cures in an emotionally-infused language. She incorporated the ‘f’, ‘s’ and even ‘mf’ word at appropriate places as well. The half-Red skinned Assistant Professor’s black humor conferred a reality to the data and speculations.

Rachel smiled with delight as one of her classmates asked Leona, “Is this going to be on the exam?”

Professor and Philosopher Leona replied, “It's going to be in the exam of life, and if it’s too hard or uncomfortable to learn it, you’ll have to continue being a lifeless corpse.”

“But this isn’t a course in microbiology,” one of the students protested sheepishly.

“It is now. Because bugs can kill you quicker and more powerfully than drugs,” she snapped while wagging her finger. “Which I do not recommend for recreational or enjoyment purposes because the madness of being a creative soul and an effective one is best enjoyed… straight,” she advised, indulging in a laugh that loosened every knot in her stomach.

Rachel looked at Leona, seeming to ask for an explanation to the pun or elaborate on the joke.

Leona threw back one of those “when it’s the right time” answer, after which she grabbed hold of another piece of chalk since the other had worn down into dust. “Anthrax,” she went on, writing the key points about that naturally-occurring and man-made disease on the board, bold enough for anyone to reac sense her boss was watching her—the sm back of her neck rising. Through a mirrored reflection on a side panel next to the overhead, she caught sight of Ditka lurking around in the hallway. He directed one of his trademark stares of condemnation straight into her defiant eyes. This time, Leona didn't care as she continued, full speed ahead.

As Leona continued on, her voice changed, and in the back of her mind, she found herself remembering things she'd witnessed and done or allowed to be done. Her voice deepened by two octaves, she tried to cover it up with a false cough, forcing it to last a minute or two, but when she looked around, there were more alive eyes in the room now.

Half of the students, by her calculation, wanted her to continue, fascinated by her passion for science and perhaps international history. Having observed herself revealing too much to the crowd of young souls, she chose to fake another cough, grabbed hold of the microphone on the podium, and continued with a tension-driven, low voice. It was that "soft talk with big impact" speech made famous by Clint Eastwood, as well as obnoxiously sterile "professional sounding" women who were the head cops on the detective shows.

"If anyone wants to leave now, that's okay, but if you want to stay, that's okay too. I won't ask anything on the exam that's not on the handouts for the course." She looked over to see if Ditka was still watching from his hiding place in the hallway—he was gone.

When she turned to her attention back to the students, they were all standing, and in unison, applauded her.

CHAPTER 2

Carlos Fernandez walked in to his side of Room 206A, unloading his mops, buckets and brooms. All the while, he sang out a Spanish song of hope and joy at the top of his lungs.

"Shh!" Leona ordered, baffled why the batch of herbs she had gotten from the reservations was having a far better affect than the herbs she had last purchased from other botanical catalogs. Though she was thankful she'd finally found something that worked better than any of the others, she was determined to find out why, scientifically.

"Shh... Carlos, I'm agonizing," she grunted.

"Over what to eat. Yes, I can see that," Carlos countered. "You look thin as a rail, Doctor Z."

"You can't eat science," Leona replied, allowing herself a break from the work and the other agonies in her always thinking head.

"But, for better or worse, you adore me." He handed Leona a taco loaded with everything from his lunchbox. "We are both at the bottom of the totem pole in this department."

"Depends on which side of the totem pole you're looking from, Doctor F." Leona discretely winced at the excessive spice permeating her nostrils then bravely took a bite from the taco. She noted with intense internal pleasure that it tasted more like reservation-prepared banuk than Boston-baked cornbread. "Any well intended deed of defiance against evil or societal-approved always sets in motion a liberation of the Soul that is unstoppable."

"You should be a philosopher, Doctor Z," Carlos offered as he put away his cleaning supplies then checked to see if the thirty-year old scintillation counter he recently resurrected was still working. "Not a scientist."

"I thought they were supposed to be the same thing," she replied with upturned lips, lamenting the career decision she had made but still 160 percent committed to it.

"With you, being a philosopher and a scientist are still possible, because you do both for the right reasons whatever those reasons really are," Carlos replied. Rather than wait for an answer, he took a large bite out of his taco. "The hotter it feels to the throat, the better it is for the belly."

Leona took another bite, sensing Carlos wanted to continue the conversation with their eyes rather than their mouths. He looked at the notes that covered her cluttered oak desk—on top of the heap, her latest research paper, one draft away from sending in to the Journal of Neuro-toxicology. Every typed sentence was matched with scribbled notes in the margins or between the lines, which only Leona and he could read. "As an engineer and mechanic, I can't understand most of the biological terms here, but what you claim here in the conclusion section seems to be ambiguous."

"Because I'm not sure yet what the data really says, or wants to say," she replied.

"Which is because your working hypothesis is flawed?" a deep baritone voice of logical reason echoed from behind Leona. "Or the reason for asking the question is irrelevant?" Professor Doctor Ditka continued as he strode into the room with an upturned chin and smug grin. "Or you are in need of collaborative advisors who can offer scientific insights and upgrades with regard to your investigative tools?"

"And I can get more insight and upgrades by kissing more ass?" Leona snarled. She noted Carlos taking the sidelines in the game now afoot, disappearing into his pile of cleaning supplies as the illiterate janitor.

"Or perhaps with the right collaborators..." Ditka continued once Carlos had disappeared amongst the janitorial clutter in the back of the lab. The good professor took off his wedding ring then held it in place above his open lab coat pocket.

Leona speculated on what might happen if she accepted his offer for the right collaboration or what calamity might ensue if she refused.

"Maybe you'd get more funding by wiggling your ass, Doctor Z," Carlos interjected in a particularly thick

Spanish accent, made more ethnic by wiggling his own derriere. “This is how things get done in America, yes? Kiss ass or kick it?”

Leona’s tight lips gave way to a silent but badly needed chuckle when hearing the impish philosopher’s wisdom. Ditka’s didn’t.

“Mister Fernandez,” he said with a firm, Germanic sense of command with as minimal volume as possible. “The floor in the cadaver lab could do with a better shine.”

“To impress the dead?” Carlos replied, knowing full well he had as much to lose as Leona if he bit the hand that fed him.

“Or walking dead,” Leona laughed. “Which describes most of the faculty here. And the students if they’re instructed, rather than actually taught, or inspired.”

Leona and Ditka engaged in a battle of wits and wills between the eyes, with an intensity that had never been felt before, at least by Leona. She dove down deep into her core to find the strength to keep her dignity and perspective as Ditka was an expert in degrading, humbling, and self-examining souls.

With an added boost of sure-footed condescension, Ditka addressed his words to Carlos, his real intentions to Leona. “We must make the cadaver lab aesthetically pleasing to flatter the living, Carlos,” he commanded in the manner of his Prussian Officer ancestors who had more respect for their dogs than the soldiers under their command.

"And their dead bodies?" Carlos inquired with a classy bow, wagering that somewhere behind Ditka's stern, cold face was a mind and soul that still knew how to laugh. "You know, my son was a medical student in Mexico City, and did very well until he uncovered the drape on his cadaver and saw his ex-wife's face. This time I can finally win an argument with you!" he said to her.

Ditka stopped Carlos' bold intelligently-designed attempt to share his special gift of humor with a loud snap of his fingers. The professor then pointed Carlos out to do to his newly-appointed rounds in the morgue with a flick of his index finger. Ditka's face was as dead as the cadavers. The consternation in his eyes clearly revealed his intentions in the land of the living with regard to Leona were far more deadly.

Carlos shrugged "I did what I could" gesture discretely to Leona. Then he lowered his head into an obedient hunchback posture, letting Ditka look down at him while never daring to look into his boss's face. It was the kind of posture anyone with any brains did while crossing from one country to another with immigration officers who have guns on their hips while crossing on either side of the border. As for leaving

Leona alone with Ditka, that was another matter entirely. Carlos stood his ground, refusing to leave the room as he'd been commanded to do so.

"It's okay, Carlos," Leona said to him in English. "Dealing with assholes is part of my job," she continued in Spanish, a lower-caste language the high-brow Ditka never bothered to learn.

"You are sure?" Carlos grimaced then continued in his beloved native tongue "You're the only one in this department who doesn't shit on the floor and expect me pick it up, Leona."

"It's okay, Carlos, really," she answered in English with a grin fixed on her lips as her eyes continued the battle of wits and wills with Ditka. "Via con Dias. Or via con Buddha. Or, no… via con the Great Spirit."

Carlos took his broom, bucket, and mop, and left Leona to fight her own battles. Meanwhile, Leona translated what needed to be translated to the asshole, quadro-lingual Chairman of the department. "Via con means 'go with'. Con Dias—'Go with God'. Get right with Buddha, get re-connected with whatever or whoever—"

Ditka halted her metaphysical discourse with something very much from the material world—a folded file he pulled from his left lab coat pocket. He held it up to Leona's face.

When she opened it, her idealistically-based bravado turned into extreme worry. "So, half of the students want me burned at the stake and half of them want me canonized."

"Which means your teaching evaluation score is average," Ditka replied. "And to keep your job, L J Zimmerman, who never did provide us with transcripts from your high school days, nor said what the L or J stands for, you need above average teaching evaluations."

"Yeah," was all that could find its way to Leona's strangulated voice-box and defeated spirit.

Ditka inspected the lab with a cursory glance then he fixed his stare upon Leona's ass, then her legs, then her breasts. He closed the door and turned to her. This time it was with kind eyes, a vulnerable and lonely soul behind them. "I could have these teaching evaluation scores recalculated," he offered with a voice that sounded trustable. "I can do the appropriate statistics on them after throwing out the lower score outliers."

Throwing out the outliers that didn't fuck with the statistics could prove nothing new at Mass U or any other institution of higher indoctrination Leona had worked in. It was a trick many scientists did when most of the values were in line with their hypothesis but one or two of them weren't. Such was completely legal both mathematically and scientifically. Truth be told, it was something Leona had done on occasion with her own data in the lab, so that life-saving concepts could get to press and perhaps the bedsides of dying patients sooner than later.

While she considered the practicality of the various compromises for a larger good, Ditka took her hand into his.

"We have more in common than you think," he said from his heart.

"Do we?" she replied, assessing her own life baggage and special needs with regard to any personal relationship or professional alliance. "Tell me what we have in common?" she asked. "Between the ears that is?"

Ditka edged his way closer to her, explaining the rationale for each advancement as he took it. "I am a reductionist. The brain is a series of reflexes that we, in our more wishful moments, think is a soul. The seat of the soul is—"

"—here?" Leona replied as she moved his hand onto her thigh. She found his shaking Paleface hands to be cold and clammy on her First Nations skin. A warm, self-approving grin overtook her face.

"Hardly," Ditka mused regarding her proposition.

"Then maybe the seat of the brain or soul is…here?" Leona replied. She moved his hand farther up the inside of her leg. "More cranially. That there's medical talk for the head," she continued with a naturally-flowing Western drawl.

"Yes, I know," Ditka said as his hand slithered further up her leg. Some of those moves were by his initiation and some by her invitation.

A light embrace initiated by Leona turned into a tight hug then one that was unbreakable.

All the while, Leona saw more and more of what Ditka was about between the ears in his brain and soul. She knew what had to be done for the greater good and prepared herself to do it.

Ditka's breathing escalated in both depth and frequency. His penile organ turned straight then very hard as his hand moved up her dress toward her most private parts. "Yes… I see we can collaborate on many projects together," he said, his aristocratic Prussian accent sounding more like trailer park ugly. "We can forget our political, social, religious and other differences," he continued as both a dirty old man and a horny inexperienced boy. "We can collaborate… together with…"

Just as his hand reached Leona's private parts, she sneaked her cell phone out from her pocket and video-recorded the foreplay as it went into a heavy and hot fourth quarter. It captured in clear focus all relevant part of Ditka's anatomy along with hers. The price clip of the film was Ditka's face when he reached his most desired position with her.

"My God!" he screamed out. "You have a—"

"Penis, that's right," Leona declared unapologetically. "An Adams' apple too," she continued in a deep, baritone voice. She whipped off her scarf from around her neck and attempted to wrap it around Ditka for another round of passionate neuro-scientific discourse. "Must have not told you about that in my application to this department."

Ditka pulled away then washed his hands raw in the sink in an attempt to purge the smut off them. "Get out of my department! Out of my sight! How dare you—"

"Give you a reason for leaving your wife?" Leona asked as her female self rather than the "him" she used to be. She picked up the wedding ring he'd taken off his finger and assessed its economic worth if hocked then tried it on for size on as an accessory on the fourth digit on her own left hand. "Let's see, what do I want?"

Ditka grabbed hold of a scalpel from the lab bench and lunged out at Leona. She grabbed his wrist with an effortless move she'd learned many years ago and hoped to never have to use again.

"Little boys shouldn't play with knives," she calmly informed him.

"Give me back my ring!" Ditka pleaded, pinned to the wall with his wrist twisted like a pretzel.

Leona consented to the request, pushing the ring back on his finger so tight he could perhaps never take it off again.

"And that video!" Ditka screamed out. "Delete it, and I'll give you anything you want!"

Leona pondered the proposition. Potentially, she could get whatever funding she wanted now and with whatever terms she demanded. She dreamed about how many diseases she could find cures for and how many toxins she could develop antidotes for. She pondered how magnificent it would be for Carlos to have his own lab, to be cleaned up periodically by Ditka and his other Ivy League shitheads. Reality set in when the cell phone rang. She looked at the display, the text, and the sender. She hesitated, not knowing what to do or think.

"Please. I'm finished if anyone sees that video. I'll give you anything you want!" Ditka pleaded while she held up her hand as she read the text message.

"Which we'll talk about when I get back," she said. Though her voice was calm, her heart pounded out loud enough to send alarm bells down to the tips of her toes.

"After you get back from where?" he asked.

Leona found herself far less concerned with Ditka's life crisis or academic power than he was concerned about the welfare of humanity. She opened the door, snapped her fingers, and pointed Ditka out of her lioness's den. Pulling his wet pants up and covering the stains on them with his lab coat, he ran down the hallway like a scared rabbit.

Meanwhile, Leona knew she had to get home fast. She looked above her at the picture of the soul she cared for. “Paul,” she said to the photo, not believing what she had just seen on the phone message. The heaviness in her chest gave way and opened the tear-ducts in her eyes. “Why or how did you get yourself killed? I was the one who was supposed to go first.”

From behind, Rachel entered, books in her arms. “Doctor Z. I was, like, coming here to ask you about doing an independent study course with you when I ran into Doctor Ditka, as he ran into me, then ran even faster down the hall and locked himself in his office. What’s going on?”

“For you, Rachel, independent study here,” Leona answered, wiping away as many tears as she could while trying to push an even bigger knot in her chest back into denial. Upon regaining her senses and perspectives, she reached into her pocket, pulled out her lab keys, and placed them into Rachel's hand, not allowing the young student to see her face. She then filled a military issue duffle-bag with the essentials she thought she would need. “The keys to the kingdom, or the dungeon, or maybe both, soon to be if I have anything to say about it, Doctor Rachel.”

She forced chuckle.

"What's going on, Doctor Z?" Rachel demanded.

"As I said, and meant, not a Massachusetts U minute ago," Leona spat out. "For you, independent study here, with Professor Carlos, and me officially, if anyone asks."

"And for you, what's going on, Leona," Rachel asked. It was the first time she'd addressed the professor she admired without an official title.

Leona could feel a student-mentor hug about to happen. Such was the last thing she could handle. As much as she didn't want to say what was going on, Rachel deserved to know some of the truth.

"I'm going back home to deal with the death of my brother. I'll be in touch as needed."

With that, she packed the remainder of her essential belongings and walked out the door. The pit in her stomach told her the world would never be the same again for student or teacher.

CHAPTER 3

The undertaker had done a great job in preparing Paul Zimmerman's body by covering all blemishes on his face and fixing his lips with a slight smile. He'd trimmed his hair neatly into a classic James Bond cut and dressed him in a suit that 007 would have been quite proud to wear in any top end casino. Indeed, if Saint Peter saw Paul appear at the Pearly Gates, he would be welcomed in by two hot looking angels, given a martini, shaken-not-stirred, and escorted to a primo seat at the Blackjack table, where he'd win every game he played with the dealer. But Leona didn't buy into that reality, and neither did her brother Paul.

Though Paul and Leona were born of the same white mother and Cree father, Paul looked far more Indian than she did. At least, that was the case when she left the reserve a decade-and-a-half ago as Leon. Now, as she stood over his lifeless body, her heart filled with remorse, regret flowed like molten lava through her veins. Her decision to leave was far from regret, as she had to save herself and transform into who she needed to be, but now she realized, she'd missed so much time with Paul.

From around the room, people discretely whispered to one another, but Leona could barely make the words out. She sensed them pretending not to stare at her, some wondering who she was, others speculating. As she looked around, she noticed numerous plates of expensive food and drink with the Arrowhead Casino logo, indicating that was where Paul had been employed, and they were happy to pay the bill for the funeral. Such was the way the new casino did things with regard to all of its transactions, according to the intel Leona had gathered since arriving home in a new body with a new name.

There was not one broke or economically-challenged Indian left on the Rez now, at least by outward appearances. Upon entering the funeral parlor, she recalled all the new split level 400k houses she'd seen as she drove from the airport. They replaced the cabins, trailers, and shacks where most of her fellow band members had lived ever since they were vacated from their teepees.

Outside those new dwellings were not horses for the summer or sleds for winter, instead, new cars, cars even she couldn't afford. It was no longer the same place she'd grown up; in fact, there was no resemblance from the past or culture. Not a single item said "honest Injun Native American" or even "no bullcrap cowboy", except for the occasional man wearing $400 cowboy boots or women strutting around with Native-design jewelry in which store-bought diamonds and pearls replaced Great Spirit blessed stones and rocks.

Leona felt as out of place here as she did at faculty mixers back at Massachusetts University. She stood out like a sore thumb in the traditional buckskin dress and brown bead-work shawl that complimented her long black hair, accessorized by moccasins that had been walked in by two generations of healers before her—given to her long ago by Edna Thunder Cloud, otherwise known as Granny.

Granny turned up to the funeral as herself, all ninety-eight pounds of her. She looked the same way as her Great Grandmother would have appeared when her village was encountered by the first Paleface who hailed from distant lands where the sun rises. Granny was ignored by the mourners as much as Leona was. No one seemed to notice the old woman, so she walked around as if she was in her own universe. From that universe, she was the only one who recognized Leona, and the only person in the room who seemed honest with herself.

There were many mourners in line with Leona to give their last respects to Paul. Some seemed concerned, others procedural, and most seemed guiltier rather than mournful. Such was one of those intuitive logically-un-provable-as-yet feelings Leona got as she took her place on line to say goodbye to the brother who she'd abandoned all too easily so many years ago. The thought emerged in Leona's aching head—if she'd have checked in with him sooner, even for a "brother to brother-turned sister" argument, he would still be alive today. Or would he? It all seemed too suspicious, and there were so many questions that demanded answers.

W*hy did our parents wait two days to tell me that my brother was dead? Plus, it makes no sense that the most stubborn man I've ever known, whose survival instinct was stronger than mine, would've killed himself.*

Not believing her brother would have committed suicide, she looked around the room for her mother or father and for some kind of explanation that made sense. She understood that statists show First Nations people were three times more likely than any other racial group in the country to kill themselves, an accepted statistic White sociologists taught in schools as genetic fact. She, herself, on several occasions had considered an exit from life stage left without leaving a goodbye note. But she and Paul had the best genetics possible, at least according to their mixed blood parents, and they both agreed, if life's journey had brought them to the brink of self-destruction that no matter where they were they could rely on the other to talk them off the edge.

Leona looked into every corner of the room to see if her mother and father were there, but they still were notably absent, maybe because they knew she would be coming. They hadn't answered the phone when she'd tried to call them back after they'd sent the e-mail about

Paul's death. All she knew for certain was the write up in the local newspaper said Paul had died after finishing his shift at work at the Casino in a car accident while driving alone. Anyone who knew him was very aware of his fear of getting behind the wheel; if he couldn't walk, bicycle, or ride a horse to work, he'd turn down the job. When she inquired about the how and where, no one would look her in the eye when delivering half-truths, as if she was a stranger. Such was understandable, as only people on the Rez she'd told about her transition from being Leon to Leona were Paul, Granny, and the mixed blood couple whose womb and sperm made Leona's birth as Leon possible.

From her place on line with the other mourners, she looked across the room for her parents yet again. Maybe they were still mad at her because of the way she'd left as Leon. Or they were, rightfully so, enraged at how she'd neglected to check in with home on any regular basis when she was off seeing or transforming the world. But today was about Paul, not Mom, Dad, herself or even Granny, the Elder who was not related to her at all, but connected to her in more important ways. They were separated by a mass of murmuring people looking important and talking.

Granny pointed to Leona's boobs, asking with hushed words if they were real.

Reading Granny's lips, Leona proudly mouthed "finally, yes" in English then Cree, with an enthusiastic thumbs up.

Granny pointed to the intersection between the upper part of Leona's two still-standing and still-defiant legs.

Leona replied with a "not yet" shrug and apologetic smile.

"That's okay for now," Granny mouthed in Cree.

Leona had kept up communication with Granny during her two decades long sabbatical from the Rez. She'd written her letters in English with whatever Cree she could remember or find on the Internet. Granny's replies would always be brief and in both languages. They were always appended by inviting Leona to come back home, even though there would be very few who would welcome. Now, paradoxically, she felt as unseen by the people she grew up with as a fly on the wall. She felt insignificant in their eyes, perhaps because she looked nothing like Leon. Or perhaps it was because she was more Indian than anyone who'd stayed on the Reserve. Or perhaps it was written in the Arrowhead Casino protocol manual that you only smile at strangers if it looks like they have lots of money they want to spend.

Leona felt one set of eyes looking at her. It was a tall, large-framed White man, a Catholic Priest, consoling a sobbing First Nations middle-aged female parishioner. He spoke with a heavy Moscovite Russian accent. It didn't make sense, as Catholic Priests in very Eastern Orthodox Moscow were as rare or absent as Mozart scholars at a Punk Rave. Every time Leona felt another alarm bell about the authenticity of this man of the cloth, he directed at her another quick yet assertive "what I am and what is going on here is none of your business" stare back at her.

Her suspicions about what was not right with this Priest were replaced by rage at what he was when she recognized the woman he was attempting to console.

Jackie Winterhalt had been an Indian Princess Homecoming Queen twenty years ago, with whom the then dumpy-looking Paul yearned to have a date with or perhaps get one sincere smile from. Jackie was now fifty pounds heavier and a heap uglier, both between the ears and below the neck. By the way she looked at his lifeless body, it seemed she loved Paul or wanted to. Her face revealed more tears than anyone else in the parlor. They seemed to be very real, as did the way she clenched the crucifix around her neck with her hand. With her right arm, she clung to the Priest in a desperate embrace.

Before Leona could pull away from what she thought was an unnoticed glance, the Priest shooed off the vagabond 'Pagan' Leona with his angry eyes, blasting out a final warning to her as he continued to console

Jackie. "Paul Zimmerman was a Christian man, as you are a Christian woman. A God-loving man. A God-fearing man, who knew the only way to the Father was through his Son, Jesus Christ. Savior of us all," he said to the ex-Druid beauty queen.

The Priest's heavenly fairy tale was a lie, as Leona felt it, and as Paul had believed it, but Jackie seemed to need to believe it. If he really was a Priest, it was his job to say pass on un-provable heavenly fairy tales as irrefutable truth. While doing so, he sneaked a look at his watch to note the time. With a calm, procedural voice, he gave Jackie a blessing then invited the next mourner to be consoled by him. He directed more mourners closer to the coffin in front of Leona. Clearly, he was doing whatever he could to ensure there were even more people in front of her, separating her from Paul's body.

Behind her came someone even more indifferent and repugnant than the Priest. It was someone who had harbored feelings for her that she'd never resolved.

"You have a lot of nerve coming here, dressed like that!" a sixty-year-old impish woman with a dress black as a Raven's feathers, skin pale as snow and tearful eyes, blasted at Leona while still smiling to everyone else who was looking at her.

"This is a funeral, Mom. I'm half-Indian, as was my brother. As were most of the people in this room," she replied, as calmly and compassionately as she could. “I’m honoring Paul and what he believed in by coming here as I am.”

“Dressed like that! In a Pagan dress? Which is a dress, Leon! I wish it were you who’d died and not your brother.” Tears streaked her face as she turned her back on Leona.

A handsome long-haired man with very Indian features came up behind the woman. He laid his long, strong arms around her. “Your mother’s still upset with the surgery you had done.”

“Am about to have, Dad,” Leona answered the man clad in a plain black suit, who was the only Indian in the room not wearing a two hundred dollar Boland around his neck or a fashion-designer tie pushed up to the neck like a hang-noose. She looked down at the organ still attached to the junction between her legs with hatred for it. “But I haven’t had the full surgery yet. Financial considerations.”

“Thank God!” her mother, Emily, said crossing herself in the manner the Catholic teachers at the Reservation Schools.

“You’re thanking God because I’m still your son, technically, or because I’m broke?” Leona shot back, unable to control herself. She hoped the only weapon she would use would be her voice this time. If Emily gave her another one of those stares, she would not be responsible for her counter-attack.

Leona's father, Tom, intervened as the peacemaker once again. He gently put his big, strong right hand on Leona's shoulder to calm her down. Then he gently placed his left arm around Emily.

"Leona, Emily, this isn't the time."

"Its name is Leon," Emily spat back at Tom. She gave the evil eye to the offspring she'd written off years ago as both defective and dangerous. "Its name is not Leona. Both of you, have some respect for Paul here," she assertively informed her husband.

"I do have respect for Paul," Leona replied, reconnecting to the compassionate, or at least pragmatic, core inside of her. "I came here like this to honor Paul's wishes and soul."

"A Christian soul," Emily insisted as she grabbed hold of the cross around her neck, twisting it in her hand with desperation as it seemed to choke the words out of her mouth. "Who died of a… yes, heart attack," she said to herself. "The Coroner said so, so it has to be true, right, Tom?" she continued, looking to Tom for an affirmation of that wish.

Tom nodded in agreement as Emily needed to believe and as he seemed to need to believe himself.

"Paul didn't believe in Pagan magic or old Injun fairy tales, right, Tom?" Emily asked her husband.

Tom nodded and hugged her.

With a clear line of sight to her father for the first time, Leona asked him with her eyes what was going on.

A lowered head held down to his neck by helplessness was the only answer he provided. “The Great Spirit will take care of Paul better than his fellow brethren here did,” he discretely whispered to her in broken Cree.

“Paul would have wanted us to get along,” Tom said. “And for us to send him to wherever he’s going with whatever faith or magic works.”

Tom, who Leona always knew as a master of discretion, gently took Emily to another group of mourners. He then looked at the Priest and motioned his finger in a third digit salute to move the line away so Leona could say goodbye to her beloved brother.

The Priest held his ground.

“She’s an old friend of Paul’s who came a long way to say her final goodbye,” Tom related to the mourners. “Please.”

Maybe it was what he said, or who he was, or which of the mourners Tom looked at first. In any case, they all moved aside. The well-dressed Priest gave him an angry “we’ll deal with this later, peon” stare, folded his hands behind his back turned his head, and strolled in the matter of an aristocrat to minister to more peasants.

With the line cleared away, Leona seemed reluctant to go up to the coffin. It wasn't because of the stares she received from people she'd known in the past but didn't recognize her now. Most of them looked at her as if she was just another drunken squaw fresh off the bus after being released from a rehab facility, but this was something she sort of expected. What surprised her was, there were two gentlemen who eyed her as if she were familiar. But, as she watched on, it occurred to her, they were mostly the married men who were more interested in a new mistress who didn't blimp out like their once-attractive trophy wives did.

Leona postulated that she reminded them of the dream babes they could have married but didn't. It was an occupational hazard of transitioning when deciding to come home. What concerned her most was a herd of well-dressed white mourners on the other side of the room, who seemed to have Eastern European faces and mannerisms, all of them hiding as much under their coats as behind their over-confident, secretive eyes. *No, I can't let myself be distracted,* she told herself as she walked slowly to open coffin. *I have unfinished business with Paul.*

Ten feet in front of the corpse, she hesitated. A cold, numbing wave of terror overtook her, shivers tingled up and down her spine like she'd never felt before then she turned away from Paul's face before she could look at him.

From behind taller "important" people, Granny nodded a suggestion for her to face her brother, her past, and perhaps her Maker. The old coot appended it by mouthing "Talk to his soul, now!" It was a command Leona wished she could disobey but couldn't.

On the way up to the coffin, she kept her eyes wide open while trying to get a glimpse of what people were looking at through the series of mirrors in the room. Yes, men were looking at her with yearning, once-attractive Injun princess Jackie with envy. Yes, the white mourners, especially those in Church going cowboy attire, were mumbling more among themselves in Russian and other European languages. As predicted, the Priest's coat, as he passed by her, smelled of extractions from female as well as male reproductive organs.

Ignoring all those most probably relevant distractions, she laid her hand on Paul's arm. It was ice cold but was certainly not the first time she'd felt the chill of dead human flesh. *Dead is dead,* she knew from her tours of duty overseas as well as her having to teach anatomy to medical students at autopsy room at Massachusetts U. *The soul vacates the body as soon as the heart stops and the brain waves go flat,* she tried to tell herself. When she looked into Paul's very open eyes, another theology entered her brain and soul.

She knelt down next to the corpse and, in Cree, delivered a prayer to him and the Creator. It was improvised in parts, but Paul would understand. Maybe the Creator was back from His or Her lunch break. Most certainly Granny, with the kind of ears that could hear a crow cawing in the woods a mile away while trucks were zooming past her at full speed on the highway, would correct Leona for her mispronunciations later.

As the prayer became a song, Leona burned sweet grass over Paul. Halfway through the half-improvised and half-recalled whispered chant, she was pulled into another perspective—her stare directed at Paul's body rather than spirit. He'd been artificially-altered to look "A-okay", but the aging lines around the lips and ocular sockets were not consistent with the rest of the face. His eyes registered fear. His face telegraphed terror, and underneath the foundation plastered on his wrists and ankles were rope burns. The suicide slashes on his wrists were either painted on or placed there long after he died, and not in the location where they would have torn open blood vessels. Under his sleeve were injection marks, which indicated the doctor who made them had a very non-compliant patient.

As for Paul overdosing himself with dope as so many Natives did on purpose when sober or by accident when drunk—her brother had kept his body clean of all foreign substances. Indeed, Paul was so afraid of drugs as a kid that he never even tried weed, despite Leona, when she was Leon, trying to cajole him into not being such a coward with regard to letting pharmacological agents give new insights. Inside his mouth was the smell of mouse, reminiscent of hemlock. As for the injected toxin, that would require blood work, which she could not do since he'd been embalmed. Taking samples from the chest and abdomen would have to be done discretely, and sent to a lab far, far away for valid analysis.

Through a mirror, she noticed the Russian cowboys talking with the Tribal Police. All of them looked curiously at the strangely attractive, familiar-looking Indian chick who was lingering at the coffin longer than they were comfortable with. With them were attractive younger women who had lifeless faces and hopeless eyes and wore jewel encased, high fashion leather-metallic choke collars that gave them a sensation of pain every time they looked at Leona or at a man other than the one they were with. Two of the women were Native American, the other three were not.

From a slide glance, she noticed the men had guns; it was a wise thing to move on to what she could do something about. She was armed with the painful knowledge that Paul had been murdered, and the conviction of his death was only the tip of the iceberg of something very evil, which had taken over the Reservation she once called home. She knew before going anywhere else, she had to put her former house and teepee back in order, no matter what it took. It was for more than just her own tribe now that was in danger of extinction or worse.

She caught a glimpse of one of the girls, a slender red-haired, Paleface beauty no older than fifteen, who was made up to look like she was an established, and legal, twenty-something. When her uncle wasn't looking, she lowered her scarf and collar, pretending it was hot, turning the view of what was underneath the latter to Leona. Then she braved a long stare into Leona's eyes, hoping she could do something about what was underneath it.

Leona didn't recognize the Satanic-looking brand engraved of the fully exposed metallic collar, but she no doubt knew what it was used for. It was confirmed when the bearer of it was called back into obedience by her uncle, one of the Russian cowboys, who saw what she was doing and pressed something in his pocket. The electric jolt shocked the red-haired beauty back into a state of submission. The size zero red-haired niece re-wrapped her fashion scarf over her neck and limped back to her owner with as a seductive gait, asking him to forgive her for her transgression.

“We’ll see,” he said with his cold, indifferent eyes.

Leona considered what to do, not having a plan in mind yet. She was now determined more than ever to get to the bottom of whatever was going on. She perused the room as discretely as possible, taking in as much data as she could with her racing brain and quick glances. She felt pulled back to the world she entered after leaving the Rez. It was the kind of realm she never talked about with her family and would never talk about to anyone on the legal side of the law.

In her former life as Leon, he’d been a good soldier when he signed up for service in the regular Army to see the world and maybe make a difference to it. Leon was an exceptional soldier when he was admitted to the Special Forces program after he displayed an intelligent set of reflexes in combative situations. As a very unofficial soldier, he had accepted the offer to work for contractors the U.S. Military paid off in hard, cold cash. On good days, Leon thought he was doing good for the world as a necessary evil, working for rich dudes whose PR people painted them as liberators forced to work outside the law. On bad days, Leon absorbed what his duty was as a hired soldier, focusing on doing right by his buddies in the field instead of concerning himself with world politics beyond his control.

Those worlds were about fight or flight, depending on the circumstances.

Leona's head abruptly got re-infused by the most horrifying of those circumstances. Just as the pictures of the movie in her mind she'd yearned to forget, appeared in acquired form, color and crystal clear sound, she felt a hand on the back of her shoulder. Perhaps it was a real hand. Perhaps it was one of those ghosts and demons that haunted her in the nightmares she had every time she tried to get some sleep and lingered around when she was awake as well. This time, she wouldn't run away or go ballistic. Renewed with the strength only she could provide from her innermost core, she turned around, prepared to stand her ground against the demons.

The intruder smiled, all ninety-eight pounds of her. "We both need to do what we have to do, together this time," Granny said, after which she handed Leona a business card. With that, Granny shuffled out of the room as unnoticed as when she was there.

Leona looked at the card and the face on it smiling back at her. The graphics on the Arrowhead Casino card, redeemable for ten dollars of White Wampum to its bearer, portrayed a welcoming Indian Chief in full headdress. His face was warm, kind, and inviting. There was only one problem: his facial structure was very white. After one deciphered what had been photo-shopped after the initial picture was taken, the face was ominously familiar to both Leona and Leon. Then again, every demon looks familiar when found stuck in hell trying to rescue those pulled into the murky, smoke filled pits.

CHAPTER 4

After being displaced from their ancestral land in Georgia by President Andrew Jackson on the infamous Trail of Tears, the Cherokee made a remarkable comeback. Adjusting to the treeless and arid landscape West of the Mississippi, they became one of the biggest producers of wheat and livestock, making them rich in Wampum, pride, and, because it just happened, Black slaves. Of course, the slave they wanted most to be working their fields was Andrew Jackson.

There were many green and white portraits of the Ex-President exchanging hands in the Arrowhead Casino, an establishment where most every family on the Rez had someone working. It was littered with white patrons who loved the spectacle of it all, and Asians obsessed with staying at the gambling table as long as their luck held up. The evenings were monitored by Eastern Europeans trying to look like cowboys or Indians, and Indians trying to look like white Russians. Each of them had a fake niece half of his age on his arm. Oddly enough, very few of the nieces were Indians.

From behind a blonde wig with big hair and matching Niemann Marcus neuvoriche “mob moma” suburban Log Island outfit, Leona observed the plethora of young adults she’d known when they were kids, who were no doubt bringing home more Wompan than their parents were able to. By the bright teeth-revealing grins on their faces, they seemed to feel good about their jobs. Truth be told, Leona knew if they didn't gleefully accept offers for employment, they would have joined the forty percent of First Nations who had no jobs to go to in the morning and a bottle of booze to keep them going till the end of the day or the end of the life. Though these good looking, seemingly happy Indians were serving drinks, they didn't look like they were consuming them. So it seemed to her in the light from the lamps atop the ceilings in the building, which had been a storage barn back in the 1880s now a rehab which had been expanded as a place of businesses. But for who? And how?

She sashayed around the tables in man hunting mode, keeping with her rich divorcee Big Crab Apple cougar persona. While pretending to eye young man meat with her ever-moving head, she peered through her over-sized imitation silver-studded sunglasses. With long stares directed from the corner of her eye and a mind that could calculate numbers faster than any sleazy used car salesman, she took note of the many money trails between the customers at the tables and the house. A quick calculation said it was more or less an equal exchange. Such was, something that no legitimate casino could sustain, unless of course the real business had nothing to do with blackjack, poker, or selling watered down booze at non-watered down prices.

It was in keeping with the promise of the Arrowhead Chief's picture on the wall pledging that in his house, "The customer always leaves a winner." But with what goods? Granny, who'd sent Leona to the Arrowhead, was notably not there. She'd not answered her phone when Leona called.

From her "Wild Bill Hickock" booth in the back of the casino, Leona continued to observe the room, trying her best to not be noticeable.

"I'm waiting for someone and will order a drink when he comes," she said to a young waiter.

She busied herself with her phone, pretending to text her date, all the while trying to send a text to Granny. *What am I thinking? Granny would never learn how to text, and if she did, she'd send messages to the guys operating the satellites above the clouds and tell them to look into their own souls instead of poking their noses into everyone else's e-mails, for national security of course*, Leona told herself.

Then it occurred to her, Granny was as inept at cyber communication and skilled at the art of soul-based eye-to-eye socialization, but she knew more about the world below the satellites than anyone. So Leona knew there was a reason Granny had her taking on this mission solo. The childless woman known as "Granny" to everyone on the Rez since they were knee high to anything, was always good with numbers, and till now anyway, had been the most valuable book-keeper for all of the businesses. Leona recalled from her writings on paper (rather than computer screen) letters with Granny two years ago, that the old woman had taken on the job of being the bookkeeper for the new Casino. *Whoever takes it over knows how to make money at the expense of Palefaces who enjoy losing it but doesn't get greedy enough to steal anyone's last dollar at the tables. But losing money up front is the easiest way to the poor house for everyone involved.*

Two things were very wrong here, Leona sensed. First, by rough calculations, ninety percent of the customers at the gambling table were taking away far more than they wagered. Second, the white uncles with the nieces took away far more than any players, with the exception of stag businessmen whose movements and attire indicated they were here for business rather than pleasure. Only finding out what was behind the doors in the back of the Casino, guarded by large framed men with red and white skin, would tell. Leona didn't know any of those men, but knew she had to, anyway she could, and without any help from Granny.

Endowed with features and perspectives half-Indian and half-white, she could slip between worlds quite easily. She admired her red-skinned ancestors for standing up to cannons and machine guns with lances and arrows and knew wars were won with superior weaponry, or failing that, superior intel. She'd super-loaded her cell phone prior to coming into the Rez with all of the bells and whistles with respect to taking pictures, recording voices, then checking data bases on the internet with regard to the people recorded and photographed. Those databases were accessible through the pass-codes Leona knew but never wrote down.

She strolled the room, pretending to check out the slot machines, hot looking men, and overpriced "Made in China" authentic Indian moccasins, then took snapshots of anyone or anything suspicious with the cell phone hidden in her purse. After hearing the low battery bleep on her phone, she retreated back to her booth in the back of the room. En-route, she felt she was being watched and followed, maybe it was the paranoia which kept her awake at night but kept her alive during the day in so many places where bad shit really did happen when least expected.

Cell phone in hand, she yapped away in "Longislandese" to her girlfriends back east about the Indian boy-toys she would bring into her penthouse teepee that night. She actually felt herself getting into the role and visualized being taken care of by an absent hubby who had something on the side of his own but kept the money at home with her. Then envisioned herself coming home after yet another hard day of trying to change the world to a warm hug, a loving kiss and trustable eyes instead of a dinner for one on a table cluttered with more work to do.

The fantasy about living someone else's life vanished after she calculated how she would turn yet another paradise into living hell for all concerned. The masochistic workaholic then started to cross reference photos of the uncles with mug shots of nasty underworld characters available only on several very classified sites via her database links. Before she could make any positive identifications, she was rudely interrupted.

"Miss," a tall man with a tightly-pulled back pony tail said. He extended his hand toward her. "May I look your phone?"

It was the kind of question that could only be answered "Yes, of course, Sir," to a man who was never denied any request. But he was a man, and Leona was, at least with regard to everything except the lingering vestigial organ between her legs, a highly desirable woman.

"Is there a problem?" she asked Russell Johnston, all-star athlete in every sport on the field. Russell had almost made it to the NFL as a first-draft pick from the Denver *Broncos*. To improve his chances for the next year, he had played with the Saskatchewan Rough Riders in Canada, injuring his left knee irreparably in game whilst winning the team a place in the playoffs. The team's part-Blackfoot owner then sent him back to the Rez to coach young Indian kids as well as to warn others about putting too many eggs in one fragile basket.

Russell didn't recognize Leona, despite the fact she'd played many games shoulder to shoulder with him when she was Leon. *Thank the Great Spirit for that save,* she thought, while Russell, in a fine, top end suit, continued to keep his hand out, requesting she hand over her phone for inspection.

"I need to see if you were taking pictures at the tables," he said. "It's against the rules," he continued, pointing to a sign on the wall.

"What happens at the Arrowhead stays at the Arrowhead. Please, respect your fellow customers' confidentiality," Leona read in her most obnoxiously crude Longislandese, pretending to see it for the first time. For personal reasons that felt right, but were maybe not that smart, she removed her sunglasses.

"I must have not seen the sign, sorry," she said flirtatiously, keeping her eyes directly on Russell.

Russell didn't recognize her face. *Six points for home team*, she thought. *Potential weapon for rest of game*, she projected.

Russell had a job to do, and he held firm. He insisted, "I need to see your phone."

"Sure, no problem," she answered as she handed him the phone, pressing the fake delete feature which would save the data in her special files retrievable only by her.

Or so she hoped anyway, as the new software hadn't been road-tested yet.

Russell looked at the phone. His face changed from concern to curiosity. Confusion then overtook him as he seemed to be recalling a lost memory triggered by the image.

"Yeah, I chuckle each time I see it, too," Leona quipped, while glancing at the picture on the phone. "Him and his secretary at an office party. That's him, drunk, wearing the dress, and her, sober, I think."

"The last taboo," Russell smiled, handing the phone back to her. "Sorry to have inconvenienced you," he continued. "Enjoy your stay at the Arrowhead."

"Maybe if you, eh…are still working here, I will?" she smiled back at him, planting a seed of flirtation. It made no sense for her to push her luck in the line of duty or perhaps personal passion. The knot in her stomach told her she'd put too much on the table, but after all, this was a gambling establishment. Getting into Russell's head and heart was a prize that would fulfill many agendas. She moved over, patting the cushioned seat next to her.

"You look tired. And this place is supposed to be about pleasing the customer. So, maybe you can please me by letting me buy you a drink," she asked through pursed ruby red lips and leaned forward just enough for

Russell to get a tasteful view of the cleavage between her breasts.

Russell looked but didn't touch. He replied with, "Thank you anyway," then pointed to a ring on his wedding finger.

"Too bad, but if you should ever want to remove it…" She reminded herself all of this was an act, wrote one of her many phone numbers on a napkin, and then handed it to him. Perhaps Russell was still Russell, somewhere, she hoped.

Russell picked up the napkin, considered it, and then reached into his wallet. He handed her a laminated photo.

"You, a wife, and two happy kids," she noted, regarding the picture of a worried looking woman, a fearful man, and two very joyous youngsters.

"Who I care about a lot," Russell said.

"And will do anything to keep them happy, healthy, and safe in a dangerous world," she surmised, handing him back the photo.

Russell put the photo back in his wallet and turned around to leave. Just when it appeared he was moving on with what was left of his life, he abruptly turned back.

"You do look familiar, though," he commented.

"We all do. The darker the room, the more familiar we seem to you, and you to us," Leona replied, about to phase into her next identity. Perhaps Russell did know something about what was going on between the uncles and the nieces, both on the Casino floor as well as those behind the well-guarded doors admitting special clients. Maybe he knew the real origin of the weapons three of the guards at the kitchen door were carrying. From the mirrored view of them accessible to Leona, they were state of the art pistols that hadn't made it to the gun-shows yet.

Back in the places of change and turmoil as Leon, Leona had developed an acute sense to whether someone was lying, deceptive, or just plain scared to want to know anything. Russell seemed to fit into that third category, as did most people in good places gone bad. She allowed herself the luxury of believing whatever dirty business was being done here was as a result of Palefaces with bigger guns than Indians. To be fair, people who value the lives of others they love more than lofty principles couldn't be faulted for letting fear get the better of them. But such was not so for those who were like Leona, who had far larger and darker challenges to deal with.

Bringing Leona back to those obstacles and demons was a distorted reflection of herself in a glass from a complimentary drink offered to her by a waitress dressed in a skimpy but tastefully designed Indian Maiden outfit. Its deliverer was Ashley Deerclaw, now all grown up with the kind of boobs Leona'd dreamt about having when she was a flat-chested pre-teen. They were complimented by a curvy ass, rather than the straight-like rail hips that most Indian women had.

"From the house, on the house," Ashley said with a perky smile, regarding the cocktail.

"Heap powerful firewater, Pocahontas," Leona replied in Longislandese as she sniffed the eighty-proof contents in the glass.

Ashley, who'd grown up defiantly proud of her Native heritage, seemed to now enjoy the condescending, overbearing racial slur.

Leona had her own problems to deal with; recalling the easiest way to infuriate a powerful foe was to refuse his, or her, kindness, she took a small sip. Though no stranger to weed and other mind comforting agents, she was now highly anti-booze, having never shared a beer with anyone in nearly five years. She knew all too painfully what happens as sips led to gulps leading to states of non-mind, in which Leon had done things he didn't remember and Leona desperately tried to forget.

Accepting this drink was in the call of duty, Leona told herself as the aromatic vapors of the pleasant-looking drink felt pleasing to her nostrils. *Liking this brew is something that is not so hard,* she continued as the dark brown elixir touched the front of her tongue and said "yes" to the taste-buds on the rest of it. *Jesus gave wine to his disciples at the Last Supper and none of them turned into drunks,* she rationalized until she opened her eyes and was met by a reflection of herself in the glass as Leon.

This image of Leon from her past was gaunt. It then turned defeated, sadistic, possessed by a demon. Leona's ears heard gunshots, then people screaming, begging for their lives. With her inner eye, she saw Leon realizing what he had become, overcome with guilt and terror, the bottle of vodka given to him by his closest friend before the firefight still in his bloody hand. She saw Leon's mouth open up, shocked at the mutilated bodies of the dead and dying. The souls of those slain bodies rose up like clouds forming into hellish red skeletons who echoed in unison to Leon "We are now dead, but you are worse than dead now."

The aroma of finely blended liquor in Leona's nostrils turned into rotten and burnt flesh, complimented by the all too familiar aroma of putrid blood.

"Something wrong?" Ashley inquired.

Leona snapped from the trance and sniffed the drink again. It was a mixture of rum, coke and vodka, but with some other ingredient she didn't recognize. "Who sent this over? Really," she asked.

"House policy," Ashley answered. "But if you don't want it, I can…"

She took the drink back and placed it on the tray.

"No, it's okay," Leona said, taking the drink back. Such might prevent at least one more beautiful First Nations girl from becoming an ugly Indian drunk before her time. She dismissed Ashley with a thank you nod, while pretending to take two more enjoyable sips.

Leona looked over to the congregation of men behind the bar, several of them eyeing her from their own version of mirror viewing. She wondered who was courting her, or wanted to anyway, and why. She considered how that courting could be turned into the game she was plotting in her still-sober, still-thinking, and still-alive head.

She was admittedly a slow learner in the most important lessons life and the Great Spirit tried to teach her. One thing she had learned very quickly was if something was fucked up in the short term, she couldn't wait for the long term to fix it.

One of the Eastern European cowboys next to the bar was trying to have his way with one of the nieces while watching the football game on the big screen with his buds. This niece was white, barely fifteen, and didn't fit into her sexy cowgirl outfit any more than her terrified face matched the happy pictures of previous customers at the Arrowhead hung on the walls.

With every forward pass, the Uncle's team accomplished on screen, he edged his grubby paws farther up the dress his of his under aged cheerleader.

Leona worked her way over to them, timing her entrance for when the Slavic wannabe cowboys' and gangsters' team was about to score a touchdown. She discretely grabbed hold of the fringes attached to the fabric on the young woman's dress.

"Hey, girlfriend," she said in her most tacky Brooklynese, accompanied by simulated gum chewing. "Really great outfit. Is that, like, a Guiber Jackson original? I used to design for them, ya know. Here, lemme see, lemme look at the lines, the stitchery, the…."

After the touchdown had been scored, and the mobsters had downed another shot of rock gut, the niece's uncle noticed Leona. Before he could say or think anything, he felt her presence clearly.

"Hey Guido number nothin," Leona whispered to the Uncle as she felt his scrotum. "You tell me who your real boss is, or I'll rip these balls of yours out and shove them up your ass."

While he was thinking about the proposition, and the consequences of refusing it, Leona motioned for the niece to make a beeline for the front door. She sweetened the deal with an offer of money to her for bus, cab or, if gotten to the right clerk, at the airport, plane fare. But the young girl remained, more afraid to leave than stay.

The Mobster Uncle smiled back at Leona. “She is my fiancée. From Old Country,” he boasted with a proud and confident smirk. “Who speak no English.”

“Who want no trouble.” the girl replied, with less of an accent than her fiancée. “Want work here.”

“Pleasing me and others who take care of her,” the Mobster said with a proud, procedural grin. “We are two consenting adults here, and you will be charged with assault if you don’t put your hand back where it belongs,” he continued, pointing Leona’s attention to the Tribal Police in full uniform standing guard next to the wall behind them.

Leona was a brave fighter but never a stupid one. She let go of the Mobster Uncle’s private parts, putting aside for the moment that it would save a lot of medical bills if someone ripped her own testicular tissue and associated phalanx out.

“So, what kind of leash do you have this filly on?” she continued, with a more Uptown diction to her voice. She then leaped over to the other side of the morality line, this time looking at the niece like she was a piece of marketable meat, examining rather than looking at her. “Crack? Special K? Or some new exotic dope that you got her hooked on? Or maybe she’s being a good girl to protect the safety of her kid or little sister back in the old country? Or an ex-boyfriend who doesn’t deserve to—”

"She is my fiancée," the Uncle interjected. "And you have watched too many movies. This is real life, and you—"

"Will want to do business with your boss," Leona countered. "Who keeps good kroysha, da?"

"I am Albanian, not Russian," the junior level mobster with the inflated head said with a condescending eye-roll in response to Leona's descriptor of "roof".

"Da, I know," Leona replied.

"And what else do you know or think you know?" the Albanian uncle said whimsically after being noticed and joined by his buddies from old country.

"That we all are going to be working together, very soon," Leona replied, in Albanian, one of those tongues she picked up while in the Balkans doing UN Peacekeeping duty, according to her official military resume, anyway.

"Why?" the next level up junior mobster inquired as the girl's fiancée was absorbing the shock of Leona being for real.

"Because I am a necessary evil." Leona continued, "And I know things about you, your friends, and your bosses that you don't. And I know things about this place, and its people, that all of you should."

The words were pre-rehearsed, and Leona had nearly exhausted her Albanian vocabulary. She hoped and prayed her new collaborators wouldn't pick up, as they conferred amongst themselves. Meanwhile, she had to answer the biological call of duty.

"I will be in there, while you are making the arrangements," she said in very Upscale Manhattan Madame English as she pointed to the rest room. "And you, my lovely Pocahontas," she directed at Ashley across the room. "A steak with all the trimmings for this girl, on me," she commanded in regarding the under aged, terrified niece. "And steak dinners for all of her roommates."

"She doesn't have any roommates," the Albanian mobster said regarding his fourteen-year-old "new wife". He pulled her closer to him, displaying a happy hug. It indeed was a picture of December-June romantic bliss for those who chose to look at the couple's smiling lips rather than their eyes or souls.

By the confounded look on Ashley's face observing the happy couple from afar, she knew nothing about what was behind the heavily guarded back doors leading to the upstairs offices other than what she was supposed to. All she knew was money came out of there for to cover her paycheck and always on time.

"I'll be in there," Leona said to her potentially new Slavic associates as she pointed to the ladies' room. "And I expect you to arrange what you have to out here while I'm gone," she directed at the Mobster Uncle. She pulled out a card from the depths of her cleavage, handing it to him. “Or sooner. My card. I expect to hear from you by midnight, or tomorrow I take my business to your competitors.”

She gave the next level up Mobster another card.

“Or maybe you’re the real boss who’s the balls and brains of this outfit, who I’ll be doing profitable business with,” she pledged to him with a quick smile, after which she wiggled her ass toward the ladies’ room.

Such made the niece’s husband feel small. Such was standard protocol for working your way up the ladder in that time-honored tradition of moving up by pushing others down.

CHAPTER 5

The long line outside the women's restroom urged Leona's decision to go into the men's. After slipping on a floor-length duster stolen from the chair of an Asian gentleman winning big at a slot machine, she stomped into the men's room, recalling the days of being Leon in that sanctuary. She eyed the men lined up against the wall going into their latrine and had to stop from screaming as she entered the stall and listened to the men talk about things they do to the women they've rented for their stay. One in particular milled around with his hands tucked in the pocket of his uniform pants, the name on his badge, Deputy Sheriff Stevenson of the Tribal Police.

She'd noted throughout the night he'd taken regular piss breaks, every ten minutes or so by her count. Maybe it was the coffee he was drinking or the donuts always in his mouth. But it wasn't his bladder condition that drew her into eyeing him as the first cop to employ or avoid. He seemed the quietest of his peers and the most aloof. Such was true both here and, as she recalled, when he was in his civilian black suit at Paul's funeral. In the seclusion of the stall, she could get a better look. There was something familiar about him, and it irritated her, but the fact he laughed as the men poked fun at the expense of the women, made her cringe. *You're a law enforcement officer for God sake, and you're laughing?*

In the stall, she watched the oblivious Stevenson's struggle with his jammed zipper and figured it was time to set her plan into motion and plant the microphones. A moan coming from the adjoining stall stopped her in her tracks, and she noted it was occupied by two feet with shaved legs wrapped around a set of very hairy legs. Between the heavy breathing, there was some talking. Mostly the bedroom banter dealt with promises about eternal love that would be fulfilled forever and ever, at least in the imagination of the seemingly young lovers. The aroma of love juices permeated the air blowing over into Leona's stall, spiced by cocaine-infused weed.

When Stevenson cleared his throat, both lovers quickly dressed and placed their feet atop the toilet seat. Leona saw him smile with vicarious delight, most probably as a result of fully knowing what had transpired between them. The quiet Tribal Cop seemed particularly proud of his own erect penile organ when he looked down on it, but he quickly whipped it back into his trousers when three other men came in. They were as different from each other in dress and temperament as Moe, Larry and Curly. None of these movers and shakers seemed to be anyone's Stooges.

One was a rich white cowboy from Texas oil country, according to his diction and upscale Western duds, spoke in a deep raspy country drawl as he went on about how Dallas had just lost the game to the New

York *Giants* then proceeded to complain about the coldness of the November Montana air. The second man spoke with a Middle Eastern accent heavily tinged with very proper British vocabulary, not a hair on his head out of place. The third was a Chinese gentleman who came off as humble to his business associate whilst at the same time appearing superior economically, socially and culturally, according to the tone of his subservient dialog and the way he held his eyes when his two comrades were not looking at him. The talk between the three men was brief but boastful. It was about the pleasure bargains they were getting from the back room merchandise, rating them with numbers. They never referred to what, or whom, the merchandise referred to, of course.

From the other side of the room, Stevenson appeared to half-listen to the three men as he washed his hands, all the while whistling the tune of the old *Andy Griffith Show* and eyeing the stall Leona was hiding in. His eyes lingered for a few seconds, but for Leona, it felt like five intense hours. He laid his hand on the handle of his service revolver, but before doing anything more with it, his phone rang and he left the room. The lovers in the stall followed, snuck from their hiding place, and paused to make sure no one saw them leave. Leona laughed. It was just as she'd suspected; they were both young and very much in lust with each other.

Looking at her watch, she knew she had about eight more minutes before the wanna be cop would be back in the bathroom. She had to move fast, and within seconds, she had the last piece of surveillance put into the hiding place.

She spent the rest of the night in the rental car parked in a discrete area of the lot outside the casino where she could see both the front and back doors. There was nothing particularly odd about the traffic going in and out of those doors. And there was nothing worth noting coming from the planted microphones in the men's room. Between the flushes, belches, and barfs, she heard some colorful conversations. Indian dudes told crude jokes about the white skin and white Rednecks spouting unbridled and inaccurate racial digs about Indians.

There was an assortment of attacks against bitchy women from men who were perhaps bastards or perhaps those penile-bearing humans who lost the battle of the sexes. There was no discussion about Paul's accidental heart attack or his tragic suicide. Nothing about the girls who were most probably chained up behind the back doors of the Casino when they were not being showcased by their owners. Nothing concerning other illicit trades of merchandise which made the casino lots of money behind the scenes.

Ready to call it a night, she removed the ear buds and placed them in the case that housed the listening devise and almost screeched when a flash of light was pushed into her face.

"Having car trouble, ma'am?" Stevenson asked from the other side of the flashlight.

"Yeah…" Leona replied. She faked a futile attempt to get the rental car going, pumping the gas pedal as aggressively as she could. "Damn rental cars."

"It'll work if you stop flooding the engine," Stevenson said in the manner of a true gentleman. "You get more gas into the engine by touching the accelerator than pounding on it."

Leona discretely pushed the listening device off and gently touched the gas pedal. As she predicted, and perhaps Stevenson intended, it did the job. "Purring like a kitten again. Thanks, Officer."

"No problem, ma'am," Stevenson said, tipping his hat to her.

He seemed to see through her, but before she could process that suspicion, a text appeared on her cell. *"Chief Boris will meet with you tomorrow at noon in his office."*

"No. My office," she texted back, nervously waiting for a reply. Nothing came back. *Perhaps I overplayed my hand?* She pondered as her heart pounded. *Perhaps feminine charm rather than seductive bitch mode is the best way to finally meet Chief Boris,* she considered regarding her strategy in this improvised tragic opera. *I*

wonder if he'll see what and who I really am before I see through and deal with him first. That is if he is who I fear he is.

"Something wrong?" Stevenson asked with a kind voice.

"I'm okay, as long as…" she said, stopping herself when the answer came back on her phone. *"My office then, but ten o'clock rather than noon,"* it read.

"I'll bring lunch. You bring an appetite for some tantalizing conversation," Leona sent back on her phone, noting Stevenson was looking away from the display.

"So, you're okay?"

"We'll see tomorrow at noon," she replied as a power bitch, not knowing or caring if he'd picked up on anything she'd said then drove off. From the rearview mirror, she watched him walk to a car and get in.

This Tribal Cop who belongs more on a kid's feel good cop show than the real life or death drama that's reality is probably a harmless victim in all of this, she pondered. *And if he is a puppet of Chief Boris, he probably doesn't even know it. But he seems to know a lot about me or wants to. That makes him my biggest threat or maybe my most powerful puppet.*

She wondered who else she would have to use as cannon fodder in her war against Chief Boris. As a necessary evil, she was no stranger to inflicting some collateral damage on a few innocent bystanders. However, every blow that wound up hurting the innocent, or those who couldn't face the fact they were guilty, resulted in ten blows that would came back at her one way or another. Such was the price of this perhaps most important, and very self-appointed, mission in her life.

CHAPTER 6

Anxiously, Leona paced back and forth, anticipating a successful meeting. She'd sent him another text as she drove off to have him meet her in the office she'd acquired. It would be her new branch at an old location she'd known about since she was a child but never quite appreciated until now. This time she had an assistant, a new worker who flew in especially for the occasion. She needed to keep a persona of professionalism, this way her secret identity would remain a secret. The space was nothing like the third hand residential trailer she had used in Newton, Massachusetts in the back woods when working overtime in the university lab, and it was bear of the few plants she'd managed to keep alive.

"Yeah, I'm finally back," she said to a Raven perched on Granny's medicine wheel, several feet from her. She swore it had the same scar on his left leg as the one who bid her good tidings when she left the Rez nearly two decades ago.

From her secluded location, called Thunder Mountain, she felt safe. It was a place of special power to those who could hear the silence. To those who lived in the material world, it was just a collection of rocks some deluded Pagan Indians put into a circle sometime during the nineteenth century.

"I'm finally back," she continued while perusing the rocks that all seemed connected to each other, if she listened to them. She edged her way to the outer edge of the circle of stones, considering whether it was appropriate for her to enter into it.

The Raven flew down from its perch and tugged at the bottom of her black cape. That garment was complimented by a long-flowing beaded, multi-layered dress of the same color. The avian visitor spoke to her in a language she could feel but not understand. Still, she had to go with the best guess as to what the Raven was trying to say to her.

“I know all of this Stevie Nicks, Elmira wannabe, Wicka wannabe wardrobe is black,” she replied to the bird’s inquiry. “And that it’s not traditional Cree, Sioux, Blackfoot or even Apache, but… it’s necessary camouflage for the suits who can’t handle seeing who and what I really am. And necessary bait for their boss, who… hmm, may need to be reminded how hungry he really is.”

Leona took off the top layer of the dress, leaving her cleavage exposed. The Raven cawed in approval, seeming to be impressed with Leona’s hard earned and fully-paid for feminine anatomy.

“I’m hoping he likes what’s under the rest of this dress as much as you do. For different reasons, of course,” she replied to the Raven in a trusting, jovial tone she rarely used when talking with those of her own species.

The bird tugged at the hem of her dress again. She stumbled then fell face down into the middle of the medicine wheel. Its power tingled through every portion of her body, which now felt light and heavy, both at the same time.

The Raven then cawed up to the sky.

Leona felt it to be an offering of some sort, delivered to the Great Spirit on behalf of both of them.

"Say a prayer for me," she said to the bird. "While you're at it, ask whatever is up there to give us some more help down here. Even necessary evils like me can't do everything on our own."

The bird seemed to be concerned with other matters. He flew up to the branch and seemed to see something not so good at the source of the dirt path leading to the medicine wheel. He then planted himself between Leona and that bush covered trail.

"Go on," he seemed to say to her, or so she believed he was saying.

"I thank you for forcing me to come back here," she said to the spirit in the sky and earth, then to each of the four directions, north, south, east and west according to those who lived in the material plane. She continued the dialog in the direction of the sky above her as the clouds seemed to move aside for her.

"I know I've stayed away for way too long. And I should have come back sooner. But I wasn't ready yet," she said to the Spirit in the sky, after which she sat down on a rock in the middle of the circle that felt cold on her hand and hot on her ass. Thinking she'd put aside coming up with a biological explanation for such, she continued the long put off discussion with the Almighty.

"Science says you don't exist, you know. Psychiatry says you are just an imaginary friend built on constructs of what we fear, love, or want to become. But I'd like you to exist. Truth be told, I need you to exist. Even if you don't exist, I need to be as effective an instrument of your will, or best intentions, as possible. I know Granny said this in Cree words that are not as awkward or long-winded or as non-musical as mine, that I only listened to them with half an ear when she said them, but I have both ears wide open now. And I need, no, want you to give some clear and understandable instructions to me in..." Still cognizant of human time, she checked her watch. "Ten minutes?"

Not five seconds later, the Raven cawed, pointing Leona's attention to the sound then sight of two black cars edging their way up the hill slowly but deliberately, ahead of the agreed upon schedule.

"Or… now?" Leona said to the Lord and Lordess up in the sky. "The Eternal now," she continued with a mild chuckle. "That's a joke," she said by way of explanation. "Maybe we can laugh at it later, if indeed you, they, or I make it possible for there to be a later for me."

The Raven flew in front of the lead car, cawing at it. It stopped, at his command. Three mobsters emerged. One was a Native American with slicked back hair. The other two were Slavic Palefaces with matching Slavic goatees. All were dressed in business attire black and well-armed with guns that looked light, efficient, and deadly.

The Raven stood his ground, disallowing them entry past his checkpoint.

The Native American mobster pulled back from the avian bodyguard. One of his Slavic co-workers laughed at him. The other aimed his gun at the bird, ordering it to move. When it didn't, he fired a warning shot in front of its feet. The bird held its ground, cawing all the more loudly at the intruders. The Native mobster backed up in with sheer terror in his face, falling on the ground en route back to the car. He looked Leona straight in the eye.

"This place and everyone here is bad medicine," the apparently well-paid and exceptionally well-groomed Indian warned his comrades, turning his head away from Leona's piercing eyes.

"Bad medicine corrected with good shot this time aimed at the bird," his Slavic associate boasted, after which he aimed his weapon and voice at the Raven. "Who, if he had any brains, would fly away now!"

"Leave the bird alone!" Leona heard from a man in the second car. He emerged slowly from the back seat, two bodyguards next to him, one Native and the other Slavic. "It's bad manners and bad business to kill those who are in our way when we can work around them, or perhaps, with them," he continued in a calm, collected voice.

As he approached, Leona slowly made out his features. His stride was bold. Every motion of his limbs moved was as minimal as possible. Though he was shorter than his subordinates, his black leather jacket and the way he carried his shoulders made him seem more powerful than all of them. His face was chiseled at the chin with tightly held cheekbones. His deep blue eyes exuded charm as much as power, inviting warmth when looked at in the right light.

"My associates call me Mister Petrovitch," he said with a Russian accent and welcoming grin as he approached Leona.

Leona remained inside the medicine wheel, feeling the need to access its power, wisdom, and protection.

Rather than shooting the bird or challenging it, Petrovitch walked a good twenty feet around it, tempering his own fear of the bird as best as he could. He finally settled to a spot that the bird seemed to approve of and continued to address its alluringly-clad Pagan Master.

"My supporters, fans and friends call me Chief Boris," he said to her with an aristocratic bow. "But you can call me whatever pleases you. And what should I call you?" he continued as he arched his way up to a very erect position worthy of a king or Czar.

"Leona," she replied, out of bravado or perhaps stupidity. "It pleases me to be called Leona," she continued in a voice she didn't recognize. The words came out of her mouth without pre-thinking. The worst name she could pick for this alias was "Leona", the most traceable to her secret past and secret present. Maybe it was time for bravado rather than reason. After all, she was speaking to the man whose vicious eyes were embedded deep into the photo-shopped image of the welcoming Indian Chief on the Arrowhead Casino logo. This charming boss-man seemed to be, according to all of Leona's logic and intuition, the man in charge here. Nay, he was the Mensch in Command. By divine coincidence, or perhaps pre-planned manipulation, Boris was the man who had been Leona's closest and most trusted comrade back when she was Leon, in the places where comradeships and alliances are tested hardest. The memory of those times flashed through her head.

The first frame played slow within Leona's mind was seen through the nose. She recalled breathing the hot desert air through Leon's overgrown handlebar mustache. Through the tuft of dried, snotty, sweat and bloodstained hair came the aroma of dried dust, burning wood and degenerating human flesh. Then she felt the unmistakable irritation of a sunbaked, sandblasted khaki military uniform on her skin. With her inner ears, she heard desperate cries for help from anyone who could deliver it. The video portion of the movie haunting her mind came into sharp focus, in soul piercing 3-D.

Women and what was left of their families screamed for help to Allah above after being dragged out of their houses. They were then dumped into what had been a coral for goats and sheep in the middle of the village square.

"We know nothing. No terrorists here! Just old men, helpless children, and widowed women!" the woman most conversant in English said.

"Bullshit!" Colonel Boris Petrovitch replied as he scraped the last layer of dirty, blood-soaked sweat from his brow. He nodded for his corporal to deliver a punch into the woman's belly. The first of what was to be many was delivered into her pregnant womb. After the woman restated her assertion that she or the others didn't know anything, a second punch was assertively inserted straight into her belly, to be sure that "no more terrorists or lying whores would be spawned", as Petrovitch said by way of explanation. It was all according to the protocol provided by the private company who was hired by the US army to do the kind of work that would get the Generals pulled in front of Congress for a class action dishonorable discharge and a lifetime in jail for war crimes.

"We come here to build schools for your daughters, and protect you from men who want to kill you and you give us more bullshit!" Colonel Boris proclaimed as the reason for it all.

"No Taliban terrorists here!" cried the next woman elected by the rest of her villagers to speak to their NATO-assigned liberators, using the best English she could recall from her three years living in Cleveland with her uncle. "We are not Taliban terrorists!" the second spokeswoman insisted.

She then invited every one of the others to say the same in the best English they could pronounce, particularly the ones who had children with them. Their houses had been searched, shot into, and, in some cases "accidently" burned by the "Peacekeeping" detachment after it had killed five men who were suspected of big time terrorism.

After the shooting had been completed, it was discovered the faces of the slain men didn't quite match the mug shots of the terrorist mercs were looking for. With a little photo shopping of the corpses, they would be convincing enough for him to collect the bounty money. Besides, Boris Petrovitch considered anyone who turned down the honor of being put in chains by him the enemy. He smirked with pride at the pictures of the slaughtered men, most of them not old enough to grow full, manly beards.

"You killed innocent men and boys!" the woman said with tears streaming down her cheeks as Petrovitch's men took ears, noses, and eyes from the slain "terrorists" as take-home prizes. "One of the dangerous terrorists you killed was my oldest son, who was unarmed, who you shot in the back after he tried to surrender. He is not a terrorist. Neither were any of his friends he was playing cards with."

"You are not as well trained as I am, and perhaps do not know your own son as well as you think you did, dear lady," Boris replied with a warm, fatherly voice. He took out a fist full of money from his back pocket, placing it in the woman's hand in full view of everyone in the village, as well as any potential insurgents in the hills above it. "But maybe you can tell me who you think might be a terrorist. Or know is a terrorist. A terrorist who now has you in his sites because you took money from me, an Infidel." He perused the buildings in the half-demolished village, followed by the translator repeating what he had said very loudly in Arabic. "Terrorists who are hiding somewhere here who maybe you know about, or who one of the other women, old men, or children know about. Terrorists who now have you in their sites as the first target for accepting money from an Infidel."

"You have a quota of heads to take home with you. It that it?" she challenged, discovering the money Colonel Boris gave her was as fake as his concern for her welfare, or for that matter, anyone else's.

"We have information, and, yes, quotas also," he whispered into her ear. "Ten to fifteen according to my boss' calculations and requirements. We will meet that quota by getting the answers we want out of you or any of the other women or children in this shitty insignificant village no one will miss when it's gone. Maybe someone else will tell me what I need to know."

He pulled a pistol out of his holster and aimed it at the row of captured civilians while with his other hand he did eni-mieeni-mino-mo, leaving it the Russian lyrics of the song who would be the someone else who would talk.

That lucky candidate turned out to be an old, crippled, and half-blind old man, who despite his ailments carried himself with dignity and grace. Clearly Petrovitch had him in mind as the random witness all along. He motioned for his most trusted man, the company medic and best sharp shooter, to escort the old man from the cage in which the other hostages were kept.

"Maybe he saw something, or heard something, Colonel Boris," Major Leon offered after escorting the old man across the main street of the village to the interrogation tent. "But we'll have to be effective about how we ask him."

Having spoken the truth as he knew and felt it, Leon gently helped the old man onto a chair, adjusting the bandage on his injured leg so it would cover the wound but not cut off circulation to the limb.

"An interesting theoretical idea and ideal," Colonel Boris replied, a plan brewing in his head as Leon sensed it. That plan seemed to also have been intuited by his ex-French Legionnaire enforcer and his favorite rescued-from-the-gallows ex-IRA co-enforcer, by the sadistic glow in their grubby faces.

The old man was abruptly pulled out of his chair and bandaged by the Legionnaire and Mick mercs. He was put against the wall, one gun pointed at his head, the other at his crotch. The interpreter asked him in Arabic where the terrorists were. The old man smiled, and simply said, with a calm voice, in his own language, "I don't know, but since you think I do, let Allah's will be done." He repeated it in discernible English then his best Russian.

"He's not afraid of dying, which means he's telling the truth," Leon asserted, as a civilized and thinking soldier.

"No, that means that he is lying to us!" Boris blasted out as a rabid dog. "But maybe his telling us what we need to know, or can use, involves someone who is closer to the cradle than the grave."

The Russian commander of the international unit let the business end of his rifle peruse the faces of the young women and more mature girls in the cattle pen, letting it choose the one with the most innocent face and kind eyes.

"Her!" he commanded the ex-Legionnaire. "The one who looks like she's this old coot's granddaughter."

Leona recalled how Leon had tried to stop his comrades from snatching the young woman from her prematurely-aged mother's arms. How the eyes of everyone else in his unit were possessed by the rush of dominating an already conquered village from which most of the men had died fighting for the NATO forces several months earlier. How he, on other occasions, was pulled into the Wolf Pack by the thrill of the kill, the smell of blood, and the fun of being top dog in so many other places they were so well paid to be so.

Normally, Leon would have gone along with Boris for the sake of the command integrity. Such was necessary for the sake of the mission, which was, according to his moral arithmetic, eventually for the greater good. But there was also the matter of the money Leon was to be paid for being part of this last mission in Iraq. His plan for that paycheck was that it would be sent home to help his family and friends back at the Rez where everyone was living hand to mouth. Maybe part of it could enable Leon to get a family of his own, with kids who didn't have to know anything about the hard life people had to live on the Rez. All of that was assuming Leon didn't intentionally drink his paycheck away at the bar or inadvertently lose it at the poker tables in the back room of the bars as so often happened. The collection of cash at the end of this last bloody road didn't quite materialize.

Back in the present, Leona remembered Boris ordering the former French Legionnaire and his IRA buddy to shoot the young woman to demonstrate to the old man what would happen to anyone else if he didn't talk. Decades had passed since her former self pulled the woman away from her potential executioner, shielding her, and then old man.

"You do remember why we're here, Leon," Boris said after ordering then convincing his subordinates to not drop Leon where he stood with a clean shot which they all could easily get. "You remember who really signs our checks. Or maybe you want to go back to being a beat cop in Cleveland for thirty thousand dollars a year? That is, if you can beat the charges raised against you there and which you could still be arrested for now."

"For doing the right thing," Leon replied, regarding those two still very open cases in which the right side of morality was on the opposite side of the law as well as police procedure. "I did the right thing!" Leon asserted, trying to convince himself.

"At the wrong time, for the wrong people. Who hired the wrong lawyers, who, because you saved my ass out here and in Africa, I can make things right with," Boris promised.

Leon knew when Boris made a promise to him he always kept it. They had been in countless campaigns together on virtually every continent. Boris had many talents, but his most valuable one was to remain on top of the totem pole no matter what regime was in control of it. His status as one of the most powerful unknown men on both sides of the law in Soviet Russia had held firm during the Glasnost years and lasted till the Soviet Union was no more and beyond. The desire to become richer had been replaced by a love for conquest and addiction to domination. He was doing the mercenary circuit for the adventure of it and to investigate opportunities abroad. Loyalty to his close friends always came first, particularly ones who Boris had adopted as apprentice-comrades.

"I know you can make things right for me," Leon said to his big brother Boris, knowing that he could and wanted to.

"Well," Boris asked again, as he looked at his watch then the hills above the village. "Do you want me to make things right for you back home so you can go home?"

"For a fee of...?" Leon asked, still protecting the old man and the young woman with his own body. Seeing that such would not be enough, he pulled out his revolver and aimed it at his fellow mercs who aimed their weapons back at them, eager and willing to execute them no matter what Boris said.

Boris laughed, madly and loudly. "Special sale today!" he announced, for all to hear. He then delivered the rest of the pledge in a soft but sincerely meant whisper to Leon alone. "I take care of all of your legal problems you have encountered in all places."

It was the kind of offer Leon could not refuse, as he was adept at getting himself into legal hot water as he was at saving innocent people from bad guys.

"And your family problems at the Reservation whom you are not able to take care of yourself anymore," Boris added, upping the ante. "I keep their asses out of jail and from being buried in the ground."

"My brother," Leon surmised, whispering it softly, recalling the heavy-duty charges laid by ladder-climbing Feds against Paul for his involvement in the American Indian Movement. Still, Leon held arm firmly around the Iraqi woman and old man, his gun remaining at the comrades in arms who one rash moment of conscience ago he would have killed anyone for.

"All you have to do is…" Boris offered with an

honest, and sincere smile, again taking note of the time.

"To do the wrong thing here," Leon said.

"The effective thing," Boris explained into Leon's keenly listening ear. "Allow me the pleasure of seeing you be the man I knew three geological survey expeditions ago. By… hmmm… fucking this woman so we don't have to kill her."

"Which is still an evil act," Leon shot back.

"Or making her think you will fuck her, unless that old man, who seems to be her grandfather, talks."

"That makes it an evil gesture."

"We are both necessary evils, my friend," Boris said as his final word regarding the matter.

Leon somehow had trusted Boris more than Leon trusted himself. Leon lowered his weapon then stood aside while his comrades in unofficial arms took the woman to one side of the street and stripped her nearly naked. They took her grandfather to the other side of the street and asked him more questions about what he knew about any remaining Taliban in the region.

"And now, it's your turn to fuck her, which is a great honor!" Boris said motioning with his hands for Leon to unzip his pants.

Leon delayed then refused.

"Then it's my turn to be honored," Boris said, his aristocratic face reeking of gutter ugly. He unzipped his own fly with his right hand. He noted the time watch strapped to his bloodstained his left wrist. “As I approach our dear lady there, the bait, you and the rest of our team of liberators will take note of the bigger fish up in the hills who—”

Boris nodded to his troops to take cover as gunfire from the hills poured down upon the village.

“The Taliban, who everyone said were not supposed to be here,” he explained to Leon after pushing his head and body under cover before his own.

Leona recalled how Boris always did protect his people from other people, and how Leon was always his most valued “people”. He felt the same about Boris, his mentor, and friend. On many occasions the student had saved the teacher’s ass from being fried. Something he regretted when this firefight went from being intense to ugly, for wounded enemy combatants, civilians and his fellow soldiers. All were expendable assets to the real bosses on top.

Leon found himself administering medical care to anyone in his path as the carnage escalated. He worried about Boris all along. He should have been worrying about himself. The bullets going into the wounded bodies that instantly turned dead came from many guns, very much including Boris’. Leon observed Boris laughing as he used injured men, and women, as target practice, immune from any shots hitting him. Continuing to do so, he strolled toward Leon, taking out three Taliban gunmen who were about to turn the company medic into a corpse.

Taking cover under two dead bodies on one side and what used to be the wall of a house on the other, Boris sat down on the stones that had been the village well. He pulled out a flask of vodka from his hip pocket, helped himself to a gulp, and then offered it to Leon. Something Boris had done so many times in so many skirmishes that never made any newspaper. For the first time, Leon refused.

Boris raged with anger until fear overtook him, courtesy of a large black crow that swooped down from the sky to dine on the dead body next to Boris. More terrified of the bird than the Taliban, Boris pulled back, then lay ten rounds into the crow, cursing at it as if it was a demon who was about to take over his soul. By the time the demon crow had gasped its last, the Taliban had retreated back into the hills, thanks in part to choppers from somewhere that sprayed fire their way. The surviving women and children in the now completely destroyed village went with them as did the old man. After covering the urine stain between his legs, Boris recovered his composure. He took another swig of vodka then offered it to Leon. Again, Leon refused, seeing every wounded man and woman he had tried to save was now dead.

"This means we are not friends anymore, then?"

Boris said as Leon he packed his gear and prepared to walk out into the desert to get lost in it. "But you owe me! I saved your life three times today. And three times before that! That makes six!"

"I saved your life, too!" Leon yelled back.

"With bravery and distinction," Boris said between gulps of Bolshevik firewater. "Three times. Which makes you owing me, let us see, three times. Which I will collect one day. Someplace. Sometime."

That someplace and somewhere was perhaps now. Leona noted that Boris, in the very real present day, was extremely interested in her now very feminized body. He feasted his eyes on every feature of her anatomy, from the top of her long-haired head to legs that came in and out of view through the slit in her skirt that went up to her shapely hips.

"You look familiar," he said.

"We all do," she replied as a real woman flirting with a real man. "And so do you to us, sometimes," she continued as she sashayed out of the medicine wheel, noticing Boris' interest in her alluring physique was displaced by something else.

The Raven planted himself between Leona and Boris, determined to hold back his advance. Leona's avian guardian launched out and pecked at his trousers then arm. Boris froze, displaying the kind of terror that happens to soldiers paralyzed by fear. None of his men could see it, of course, and it would be disastrous if any of them did. It would mean death to his position as Colonel or Chief Boris.

Connecting to the Lady in the sky, and the woman that she wanted most to be, Leona turned to the Raven. “Leave Boris alone. He’s my responsibility to understand or neutralize now,” she said in her best Cree to the avian messenger with a seductive tone in her most feminine Leona voice. The Raven seemed to understood Leona’s alluringly-delivered message, as it flew away on cue and in the direction she’d visualized it would. Boris’ reputation, and by inference life, was saved.

Leona counted one of the three debts for his saving her life when she was Leon as paid off. With a hard and uncertain two more to go, she motioned for Boris to join her for a private conference under a tree. Utilizing a power-Priestess flick of her wrist, and a few more common Cree words she made sound like magic spells, Leona vacated the branches above her of other avian observers. She hoped the conference chamber in her woodland office was free from any unidentified human onlookers as well.

The tree Leona chose to have the meeting under seemed much like the fabled 500-year-old oak that Hippocrates used to do most of his teaching back in Kos, a small, insignificant town relative to ancient Athens. As she sat on a moss-covered rock a few inches higher than the cold stone she had chosen for her guest, her focus gravitated onto the old Philosopher Physician who made modern medicine possible.

A brilliant dude, Hippocrates was, but would he have been a better doc and teacher if he took on women as students instead of just men? And what if Hippocrates had ventured into the exploration most men consider at one time or another—becoming a woman, living as one a short while, she considered while waiting for Boris to find a comfortable place to sit under the tree. Such gender jumps were a required education for healers in many Native American tribes before a man was allowed to treat patients of both genders. The most skilled, influential, and emotionally-appealing male actors in present times in their attempts to heal the collective human soul put on the dress, wig, and heels for performance purposes, and sometimes when the cameras were looking. Marlon Brando, Dustin Hoffman, Daniel Craig, Robin Williams, Boris Karloff and virtually all of the established and insightful edgy British comics had so proficiently and boldly demonstrated such.

Leona's major spiritual awakening occurred after she had decided to be true to the feminine side of herself, committing herself to becoming a woman in body as well as repressed and denied spirit. Those means of denial had included never allowing Leon's hair to grow out more than a crew cut after he left the Rez. Then there was all that enrollment into as many macho sports and occupations as possible. During that dark time, Leon looked the other way when a trailer for *Some Like it Hot*, *Tootsie*, or *Mrs. Doubtfire* flashed on the movie screen, or a scene from a gender bender film happened to be on the tube in a house where he was visiting.

Leona knew now, more than ever, that to be the most effective human in the service of humanity was to use all of the tools available to both genders. Right now that involved being perceived as a woman by a homophobic man who made Vladimir Putin look like a bisexual gay activist.

"Sit, please," Leona said to Chief Boris with a welcoming smile as she took her position as both entertainer and teacher. She felt as if she was channeling the spirit of Aspasia, the most alluring courtesan and philosophical educator in Ancient Greece. Aspasia's lover was none other than Pericles, the noble and freely elected mayor of Athens. His prize student was Socrates; an impish stonemason by day who never got paid a drachma for his innovative philosophical ideas and ideals. But to the xenophobic mainstream working class stiffs and stuck up aristocrats of Athens, Aspasia was a foreign-born whore Aspasia who dared to have a love affair with the very married Pericles. Being more philosophical and smart than most men, she was of course labeled a witch, a dangerous one as she mentored as many young men and women in the arts and sciences in her "guest house". The trick for women such as Aspasia to keep her school open and her head attached to her voluptuous body was to never get pregnant. As well, wherever possible, she had to always let the man in charge think the best ideas that emerged between them in discourses came from him.

Though not written in any historical text, Aspasia no doubt had her own spirit helper animals. Those "savage and ignorant" beasts in all probability taught her how to deal with the lower species of humans as well as providing her with non-competitive discourse and companionship. *Maybe I was Aspasia in a past life and you were my mentor-hawk, or maybe I was the bird and you were the brilliant philosopher whore*, Leona said softly in a mystical language of her own design to the Raven, who positioned himself between Boris' mobsters and their avian-terrified boss.

"Interesting relationship you have with the animals here," Boris said to Leona. "Is that raven a friend of yours?"

"All of the birds, beavers, and bears out here are my friends."

"So, you are a witch?" he surmised, gazing at her black dress, drawn even deeper into what was under it. "A witch who loves animals."

"Almost as much as I love money and power," she

said from a perspective that was more Leon than Leona.

"And I should let you share my power because…?" Chief Boris asked, as if it was indeed a conversation between Aspasia and Pericles.

"Because you will share your power with me and want to," Leona answered with a logical and non-offensive affirmation. "Because we speak the same language with a few variations on the diction," she continued with a warm smile. That hard-earned and seldom given grin became warmer and more inviting as she sang the Russian National Anthem in Cree.

A few of the animals joined in with the appropriate sounds which, ominously, were in the same key as Leona's melody and provided an interesting harmony. *A gift from the Great Spirit,* Leona thought to herself, as silently as she could.

Boris' men, old guard Soviets or other Eastern Block goons by the looks of them, seemed to like the singing and the harmony. That 'Oh, but for the good old days to be back' warmth came over their stone-cold faces as they melted into becoming boys again. Boris seemed to recall the good old days as well by the way he was humming along with the tune.

Leona directed the next few verses not to the sky, the birds, or Boris' men, but to him, and him alone. She stroked his arm gently then ran her fingers gently down his cheeks. She pulled away just as he was about to grab hold of her. Taming the beast, for his own good, she invited him to dance with her to the accompaniment of a song she now alluringly hummed. Leona, of course, let Boris lead but maintained enough control of the improvised movements so he would be more interested in the two mountains on her chest than the taped down vestigial cannon between her legs.

At the end of the dance, Boris was hers, for the moment anyway. “So, now we talk business?” Leona asserted, as a question of course. “In English, please. My conversational Russian is not so...dobrey.”

Boris corrected Leona’s pronunciation of the Slavic word for “good”, pointing out she pronounced the word like an Albanian. He retrieved from his breast pocket two cigarettes from an Arrowhead Casino pack that bore his likeness under the full-feathered headdress. He lit one for himself and one for Leona. Trusting there was tobacco and not some kind of truth serum it, or perhaps death serum, she accepted. It seemed like tobacco, and very good tobacco at that.

Maybe it represented another kind of business, Leona pondered, as Indians were allowed to buy tobacco at cheap prices, acquiring lung cancer more quickly as well. *And if the smokes were transported across the border to Canada through Reservations that had land on both sides of the line and no white border guards, it would bring in big profits when sold to Paleface*

Canadian smokers, she silently considered behind eyes she had trained to never let anyone see through, even if it was for her own good. *Smuggling of other goods through Reservations that were on both sides of the 49th parallel could also involve illegal human cargo,* Leona continued in the always-active silent self-talk echoing between her ears.

She angrily recalled Boris had a special interest in human trafficking, even when hired as a liberator by high level CEOs companies to extract their spoiled brat daughters from suspected sex slaves. Only now, as Leona, did she realize that those philosophical discussions about the virtues of sex slavery Boris shared with a very tanked Leon reflected Boris' secret desire to specialize in human trafficking and sex slavery when it became most profitable.

"Tell me," Boris said, as he smoked the cigarette, seeing Leona was inhaling hers as well, as Boris insisted on never drinking or smoking alone. "How it is that you know Albanian, as your Russian reeks of it?"

"Travel," she replied, knowing the art and power of keeping one's answers short, particularly when relating half-truths and half-lies. "Lots of travel."

"And the business you are in which makes this travel possible?" he inquired.

"The business of pleasure," she said alluringly. "Other people's pleasure. Provided by other people of course. Better business that way. And delivering other things to people in places where their governments don't want them to have them."

"Such as what is in that medicine pouch tied to your belt?" Boris asked, referring the Indian handbag, which was the most important part of her ensemble in more ways than one.

Leona's life-tired face eased into a satisfied grin. Boris had taken the bait hook, line, and sinker. She pulled out the traditional Cree medicine bag that matched her Wiccan outfit so well then retrieved from it five ampules of powder all with coded labels. She offered a view of those well-protected ampules to Boris, allowing him to examine them.

"Interesting scientific labels here," he said.

"For very scientifically formulated compounds," she commented. "Ricin, the most effective variety, that kills in hours rather than days, thanks to mixing it in with liposomes, which comes in a slow or ultra-fast acting form. Anthrax that is resistant to the standard antibiotics, but which is neutralized by medications I can provide for a special price to special customers. HIN1 for nuisance clients. Rinderpest that puts down people as well as cattle. And finally, the last one."

She opened up the vial, offering Boris a complimentary sample-testing sniff. By the way he was avoiding it, Boris seemed convinced the powders were real. Leona took in a whiff of the fifth ampule then offered it to her host.

"A mousy odor," he noted with a familiar smile. "For an ancient concoction. Hemlock. Which we can label, Socratic Perfume. To give as a gift to ungrateful and dangerous people."

Leona gently took back the vial of the easily prepared poison she had made the night before. Apparently, she was right about Boris having plans in mind to mix it up as death-promoting perfume for any of the nieces who knew too much about their uncles or himself.

"Socrates took hemlock after being requested to do so by his Athenian prosecutors," Boris said. "Which means that he committed suicide, technically."

"True, on both counts."

"So, are you are planning your own suicide tonight, as with all of this black you are already dressed for it?"

"Only if I, or we, get caught with these," Leona said, referring to the other vials in her bag, which for the moment, were still sealed. Thanks to the Great Spirit, he didn't open them. And thanks to the Great Spirit he still respected Leona's feminine virtue. "There is one thing that we will need for our expanding operation," she continued. "An honest Injun who can be trusted to keep the books."

"You have someone in mind?"

"An old woman who is harmless. She's been here forever, according to everyone I asked. She goes by the name of Granny."

"She goes by the name of useless now," Boris replied with a condescending smirk. "Her head can't figure out numbers anymore. Or life. Better that the crazy old lunatic lives in past when buffalo owned the plains and the only way to stay warm in the winter was to collect and burn their shit. Better for us that way. And better for her. Da?"

"Da, Comrade," Leona smiled back as a colleague with a shared masochistic morality. She knew full well Boris was capable of putting Granny in a locked psych ward if she decided to give voice to the way the world here was now, and how it should be to the wrong people on either side of the law outside of the Rez. "And I expect to hear from you about the specific terms of our new arrangement in three hours." Leona proposed. "Or in four hours I will be forced to work with someone else."

With that, she walked away from Boris and the animals surrounding the medicine wheel and got into the newly shined rental car. That wheeled getaway steed required some adjustment before visiting the next person on her list.

CHAPTER 7

It finally occurred to Leona why Granny hadn't opened her door to her when she stopped by twice before. "Clean, shiny cars always have dirty people inside of them." She recalled Granny saying that the last summer she'd spent with her. It was that critical August when she, as Leon, was considering many transitions ahead and not only dealing with gender. During that golden season of blooming cactus flowers, multi-hued butterflies, and hungry mosquitoes, Granny taught Leon everything she knew or tried to anyway.

As for this fall, the snows hadn't yet come down from the graying sky. But there was a foreboding chill in the air. Leona traded in her rental car as on a new husband or boy-toy finding expedition for someone more like herself. In her new present persona as a painter-songwriter from New Mexico, she insisted on getting the most broken down car on the lot from Rent a Wreck two towns away, claiming she liked the color of the rusted out beater whose heater made more noise than hot air. The clerk was more interested in getting into her pants than checking into her credit history or psychiatric profile after she insisted on paying cash for the rental and the damage deposit, amounting to more than the beater was worth.

As ugly as the multicolored rust-bucket looked, for

the most part it ran well, except the muffler was more ornamental than functional, creating enough noise for anyone to get out of the way or take notice of its arrival. To make it her own even more, she put stickers on the bumpers. They were duplicates of what she had on her own car back in Boston that she hoped some of her students, very much including Rachel, would put on theirs. They included, God: The mystery no one really knows; make love not lust; and no such thing as too much intensity.

She tapped three times on the door.

"I was wondering when you would get here," Granny said to her with a shotgun under one arm, a handful of sacred sweet grass in the other. "That is if you are who I think you are."

"It's me, as you well know," the corner of her mouth curled as she replied. "The freak who used to be Leon."

"And now you are someone… truer to yourself."

Granny's stern face eased into a warm smile. She lowered the business end of the fifty-year-old shotgun that was adorned and empowered with beaded fringed leather that looked like it was old enough to have been used at Little Big Horn.

"Astom," she beckoned, waving Leona inside.

Leona, clad in artist clothing that was part Santa Fe chic and part Albuquerque real, hadn't heard "come" said in Cree in a long time. Granny had a way of making it sound more like “welcome”. Leona hadn’t felt really welcomed anywhere in a long time.

The inside of the shack was just as she’d remembered and hoped it would still be. Every inch of shelf space was occupied by something from the earth, honoring it one way or another. Prominently featured were the herbs Granny was presently using to concoct healing medicines. Faded, weather-beaten photographs on the wall showed the glowing faces of those she had healed over the decades. Leona recognized her own picture as Leon among them, along with Paul. It was the photo showing both lads atop horses with big fat confident grins on their faces.

She allowed herself to be absorbed by the memory of that golden summer of exploration and discovery, when things between her and Paul were the tops. At that time, both siblings were on the best of terms with their father, a radical American Indian Movement activist. Things were also good with their mother, then a white hippie who truly did embrace the gentlest aspects of the all you need is love sixties. Most everyone worked various odd jobs during those times, even though very few Indians or half-breeds were allowed to work at high paying positions in town. Anyone who mattered knew that broke was a state of economics, and poor was a state of mind. No one at that time on the Rez was poor, most importantly, Granny. She wore her second-hand jeans, hand-me-down leather fringe coats, and hole-ridden moccasins with the pride of European royalty both then and now.

Leona stepped into the kitchen area of the cabin, drawn to it by the aroma of her favorite tea and sort of most favorite brand of Granny's bannock. The old woman who never surrendered to old age went on with the job of preparing an herbal remedy for body, mind, and spirit, custom made for another confidential customer who the doctors, shrinks, and priests could not help. "So, how are you going to stop these Russian Palefaces from taking out dignity after the American Long knives took our land?" Granny asked her. The old woman allowed the young one to ingest two sips of tea and three bites of the Saskatoon berry containing homemade banuk.

"I don't know yet," Leona answered. "But by the berries in the stream and the green corn in the ground, I swear to not let anyone else to steal or buy our dignity," she continued in Cree with a clenched fist, looking yet again at her watch as impatient as she was now intense.

Granny laughed.

"What are you laughing at?!" Leona grunted back in her father's ancestral tongue.

Moving away from her herbal preparation counter, sensing Leona needed her full attention, Granny hobbled over to Leona and sat in front of her. "You meant to swear by something else, I think," she said with her usual kind yet always assertive voice in English. "Your Cree is very rusty. Maybe because of all of those new poisons from sterile bottles you've been studying and taking."

"Medications, Granny, for my transition," Leona said, holding back the rage in her gut with a lump in her throat. "They are scientifically-formulated medications. And, besides, I'm a scientist now," she asserted with pride. She looked at her watch again. The timetable in her head told her that soon the call from Boris would come in, and he would not be in the best of moods. She was thirty-six minutes late with regard to getting the intel from Granny to most effectively handle that call. "Yes, I'm a scientist now," she answered with a more respectful tone, checking her watch yet again.

"Who now tells time according to an overseer you've shackled on your wrist," Granny spat out. She ripped the watch off Leona's arm, and threw it across the room. "You should expand your measurement of time and your research beyond Palefaces' agendas and limitations," she continued. "Heal yourself before healing others, Professor Doctor Leona," she added. Granny followed up on the offer with a heaping tablespoon of the herbal concoction she'd been working on since Leona entered. "Two pinches of this under the tongue, one on top of it."

Leona smelled the medicinal powder, finding it as

displeasing to her nostrils as Granny's digs aimed at her self-taught Internet Cree was on her ego. "What is this?"

"Something to open up this," Granny replied, pointing her shriveled up arthritic index finger at the point between her two tired, burnt out but still defiant eyes. "Like you becoming a woman opened up this," the Elder continued gently placing her open palm on Leona's heart. "Which will open up this," Granny said in that "I'm sure it will work because it has a thousand times before" voice of hers pointing yet again at Leona's third eye in the middle of her forehead.

Granny's touch always felt weird, but now it felt electric. It sent a soul-awakening chill through Leona's arms and legs. Leona considered taking Granny's special very non-scientific and most probably FDA non-approved medicinal, but she was still reluctant. Maybe it was because Leona knew too much about biology now. Or maybe it was because those stories about people getting screwed up by Granny's medicines that Leona's mother wrote to her about really were true. After all, her body was still in transition with at least five female-promoting hormones, requiring a strict and carefully-regulated regiment of medications so that stroke, heart attack, osteoporosis, diabetes, and any of four kinds of cancer didn't materialize unexpectedly.

"When you were a young boy, you used to trust me with everything," Granny lamented.

"And I still do," Leona replied, staring at the space in front of her eyes and the memories brewing inside her head. "With what matters."

"And what matters most is what, Leona?" Granny asked, allowing her prodigal student to determine where the lesson would go next.

It wasn't how Granny asked the question, or what it was, but how it was addressed that mattered most to Leona. "I meant to say something earlier, but thank you for calling me Leona," she said to the old woman with gratitude. "Not Leon."

"That's your name now, isn't it?" Granny replied. She then growled at her two gnarly feet, commanding them to carry her to her workbench up a small flight of stairs, despite the severe arthritis pain that got worse with each step. "You aren't stupid, tacky, or cool enough to have named yourself something like Ashley, Bree or Krystal with two ys and three ks," she said to Leona, en route insisting that she made the journey alone. "Gotta be who you are. No, even as Leon, you were Leona. And that is who you are now."

"Not according to my family and friends, who either don't recognize me now or turn their eyes away from me when they do," Leona spat out with tears of hurt held behind her eyes. "Narrow minded idiots and assholes. Fucking apples."

"Red on the outside, white on the inside," Granny

lamented through a cough, an expression of body malfunction, which Leona had never heard from her. "Yes, I know, too many apples," Granny said, just as Leona was about to ask the old woman about her health.

"And the Band cops?" Leona inquired. "Who were supposed to be protecting and enforcing our laws?"

"But not our principles or morality," Granny replied. Her sorrowful face turned beet red with anger. Her gentle herb-cutting hand turned into a clenched fist that grasped rather than just held the knife handle. She directed her righteous indignation at the plants, demolishing them into powder, mixed in with a small amount of blood from the cuts she made in her fingers. Still, she remained quiet about the details about what was really going on at the Rez.

Leona brought up one of those details, the one which brought her out here. "My brother, Paul," she said, thinking it was the best strategy to make Granny's heart, mind, and brain all agree to open her clenched mouth. "Who was the first person, other than me, to see me in a dress? And didn't look at me like I was a pervert or sick in the head for needing to wear it. What did he know or do to get him killed?"

"What's going to get you killed if you don't leave here while you can," Granny warned. "And about your brother, there are some things you should know. Which you will find out, in the right time."

"I'm a necessary evil! Who needs to know what he knew and did and was. Now!" Leona grabbed hold of the watch Granny had requested she take off and strapped it tightly on her wrist. Upon looking at it, she realized that time had passed faster than she calculated.

"And you need to know what you think I know," Granny said, coughing once again. She looked at all of the photographs on the shelves and the walls. She seemed to be recalling the fond memories she had with the kids who allowed her to be the kind of parent they could never have at home, as well as adults who needed a good and tough friend. "Up here on this mountain, they call me Granny, still with respect to my old tired face. But behind my back… well…" The demons of old age seemed to have caught up with the old woman, about to corner and devour her into their vortex of defeat.

"They think you're harmless," Leona put forth. "Finished. Washed up. Helpless to do anything about anything."

"Which maybe I am… now. Harmless," Granny said with a hopelessness and helplessness Leona had never seen in her. Something had happened between the time Leona spotted her at the Funeral Parlor and the time Leona went to the Casino where she thought Granny would meet her. "Yeah, guess there's a time when we all become harmless and helpless."

"Well, I'm not harmless or helpless," Leona asserted, forcing her face into Granny's downturned eyes. "And you shouldn't be either! Paul wouldn't want us to be. And what about the enslaved girls who are living as walking corpses now under Chief Boris' care? How many and where they are I don't know yet. And what about the people elsewhere who will be killed by the guns, chemicals, and germs Chief Boris is probably selling that the highest bidder can kill whole populations of people whose only crime is that they want to continue living another day? What kinds of weapons and where they will be used, I don't know yet. And—"

Granny raised her hand, requesting Leona to stop relating the details. "I know," her voice quivered, tears streaming down the wrinkles in her weather-beaten face.

"So," Leona said, feeling somehow Granny had instantly promoted her to the status of an Elder before her time. "It's a good day to die?" she continued in Cree, saying that battle-cry with the conviction of Sitting Bull, the passion of Crazy Horse, and the confidence that Granny emitted every time encouraged others to do something expansive that was also scary. Such had included Granny making you get on a kind horse that was still a bit too green. She also would intimidate you into climbing up a mountain when you were afraid of heights. She'd assertively cajole or give voice to song on stage at the Rez talent shows even though you felt intimidated by the cool kids who had more fans.

Granny answered Leona's challenge with a smile then and a restatement of those immortal words. "It is a good day to die," she with more depth than Leona ever heard from that phrase, in Cree. "And a necessary day to make these fucking legs of mine do something useful other than just reminding me that they're arthritic," she continued in English.

Granny hobbled down the stairs to a padlocked footlocker buried under gamey-smelling hides and locker-room scented underwear. She reached into the very private parts between her legs and pulled out a key then opened it. With reverence and terror, she took out a ledger and handed it to Leona. "The real accounting books for the Rez before Chief Boris came, while he was building the casino. And everything that went on there until two months ago when I was asked to leave because of my sudden onset of probably unnaturally-caused bad health," she said.

"Or what would happen to your health if you didn't leave," Leona surmised as she opened the ledger to the first page, which looked at first glance very different than the last ones.

"What's in here doesn't exist," Granny said, after which she coughed up blood as well as phlegm. The breaths that followed sounded like a death rattle. Leona, as Leon, had heard that harbinger of doom all too often in places that Granny or most anyone else in the safe countries of the world did not know about, and she couldn't tell them about. "Do what you have to with it," the old woman commanded. "And only with people you trust."

"Which is you, who I will see tomorrow, yes? Like you always told me, Nature never gives you a problem without a solution. Isn't there something in this cabin that you can use to cure yourself?"

"Nature doesn't work that way," the old woman replied with peaceful resignation as she observed skin around her thin arm bones twitch un-controllably. "Not with whatever I got, anyway."

"Which I can stop, and will make disappear!" Leona asserted. She placed her hands over Granny's shaking limbs and then did a quick neuro exam. "My prize grad student, Rachel, who I fear is cursed with being my protégée, can send out meds from my lab that is still in the experimental stage, but they're effective. And if they don't work, my friend Carlos can make a midnight deposit from the University Pharmacy on his janitorial rounds."

"And why should they do that? Why should they get themselves and you into so much trouble?" Granny inquired.

"Because it's a good day to die tomorrow or maybe the days well after tomorrow," Leona asserted. "Right?"

she pleaded on bended knee.

"Yes, it will be," Granny agreed, sucking in the fire in her gut and forcing her lungs to breathe normally. "Tomorrow, or many tomorrows from now, will be a good day to die for both of us," Granny admonished, as she laid her re-empowered hand on Leona's shaking shoulder.

Leona let the shoulder assurance merge into a hug, after which Granny slipped the ledger into her purse. A familiar-looking horse came to the window to watch as if on cue. So many things were on cue with a script known only as the Great Spirit at Granny's house.

"That's… Wild Thunder," Leona noted regarding the old steed. "He taught me how to ride when I was a kid! By throwing me off every time I did something wrong,"

"Who's done most everything right since then," Granny replied, gently stroking the horse's forehead then solidifying the inter-species embrace by breathing into her equine companion's nostril. She pulled out a small sac of grain and then threw it on a rock next to the door. Once the horse got to eating, Granny retrieved the twisted bridle from a hook on the wall. After a third offer of assistance, she accepted Leona's offer to help her pull the saddle off a rope hanging from the wall. They both proceeded to the horse.

Granny insisted on putting on all the tack, and Leona discretely made sure that it was all secured tightly and functional. "Wild Thunder is called Gentle Rock now," the old woman shared. "Soft Mud by those who think his kindness and slowness is because he's stupid or weak. It's time I go for a ride on him, to ask the mountain about all of this. And for you to take that rental pony down the hill to see what kind of shit is coming down in the valley below."

Leona offered to give Granny a leg up on the now swaybacked long-in-the-tooth gelding. Granny stared her down then moved the horse to a downward sloping trail which allowed for easy mounting. "And if you're worried about me here, don't. Thunder has never tossed me off," Granny said proudly after pushing her right leg over the saddle, then into the stirrup.

"Because you never do anything wrong?" Leona yelled out as Granny rode off into the hill above her hut at a slow trot.

"Because he always does everything right," Granny exclaimed with the vitality of a woman half her age.

Leona feasted herself on a view of an old woman and an aged gelding who refused to surrender to age. She hoped that when it was her time to have more gray hairs than black ones, more wrinkles than smooth patches of skin on her cheeks and have to hold her head up high with a hunched up back that it would be like Granny. But life as it was called Leona back via the beckoning of the mechanical minion of evil that plant toxins into your brain as defined it anyway.

She put the cell phone to her ear two rings after she saw who it was, Boris. She answered in her best "I'm the most alluring and interesting power bitch you'll ever have the pleasure of playing with" voice. "You're calling me back early."

Boris related the time and place for the meeting, mentioning the menu options at the restaurant as enticement. Steak and crab indeed were the most favored food to Leona's palate. It was Leon's favorite meal as well. It was another so-called coincidence that told her that she was in the right place to fulfill her real purpose in life. Or she was sashaying into in the crosshairs of executioners who would make her death painful and ugly.

She calculated how long it would take her to get the eatery and the other things she had to do along the way for her own agendas. "Yes, six p.m. is it then," she said to Boris, appended with an alluring and businesslike "Dasvidania," being sure to have diction correct this time.

The road down from Granny's shack and meta-physiological laboratory was bumpier than the drive up. It was also noisier. Maybe Leona had picked a path through the grasslands that had more rocks than grass on it. Or maybe it was time for the shocks, pistons, and exhaust system to do an "it's a good day to die" defiant yelp of protest on the beater, which like all American-made cars was built to self-destruct at a time most inconvenient for the trusting buyer. But no smoke came out of the engine, and there was no indication of fire under the hood. Such could not be said about Granny's shack on top of the hill.

Leona heard an explosion far louder than a missing piston or a backfiring exhaust system. Through her rear-view mirror, she saw Granny's shack blow up with three more explosions. Barely three seconds later it became enveloped into a blazing inferno.

Rushing away from it was a rider-less Wild Thunder. The old gelding somehow found the strength and smarts to run toward Leona's car. She mounted the horse and galloped up the hill as fast as she could.

"Granny!" she cried out to the hills, hoping the old woman was still alive somewhere. She received no answer from the mountain or any of its four-legged inhabitants. Then when she looked at the shack or what was left of it. She saw a lifeless, burnt body in the brush behind the burning charcoal mound that had been her shack and never-invaded, well-hidden sanctuary. Granny's eyes were still fighting, but her Spirit had left the body. A pool of blood emanated from her left wrist, a bloody imprint of her hand on a knife in her right. Next to the body were tracks from a car. They were very fresh. With her super-human hearing, Leona heard the sound of that vehicle as it zoomed over the hills then back toward the highway. The sound of the escaping car was then absorbed into a brisk North wind that emerged out of the ominously dark blue sky.

Horror found its way into Leona then guilt. “Forgive me, Granny,” she said to her departed friend and Mentor. *If I came out here earlier, maybe this would not have happened. And if I was looking over my shoulder to see if anyone was following me, maybe I would have not led my enemies to you*, Leona dared to think, but could not say.

CHAPTER 8

"I'm sorry about what happened to your grandmother," Deputy Sheriff Bill Stevenson said when he arrived on the scene as the cops reached the tail end of their investigation. "And the way it happened."

"Suicide?" Leona shot back, seeing that same laziness in Stevenson's as in his asshole colleagues. "That would make the paperwork a lot easier for you."

Standing beside her, Stevenson offered her a cup of coffee from his thermos. Pissed off, she pushed it away, spilling it on his jacket.

"Fuck off, all of you!" she barked in Leon's voice. "Please," she pleaded after, which she faked a cough. "Just go away, please," she continued as Leona.

Stevenson wiped the coffee off his jacket with the spare bandana in his pocket then took in a deep breath. He answered her in a calm, collected voice, seeming to be more concerned with the issues of the case rather than Leona's personal history.

"Look, Leona. The Fire Inspector said the blaze was no accident, and it's no secret your grandmother had a long history of being clinically depressed. The slashes on her left wrist, the fingerprints on the bloody knife on her right."

"I know. Which would fit in very well with your story if she was right handed."

"And the peyote-laced weed in her mouth. She was

doing some heavy-duty tripping, mixed with being afflicted with mental and neurological illness that were already—"

"She would have and did endure her mental illnesses without any pharmaceutical or herbal health!" Leona shot back. "For as long as anyone knew her. She told everyone that if whatever mind-altering shit goes into your mouth to take you to a sacred or satisfying place, even blessed peyote, takes you to no place real. No place you can really trust. Visionary Madness is best enjoyed straight." She self-observed the pun and the irony of it all. "Straight!" she said, with a chuckle then a "what else do I have to lose" laugh.

She didn't plan to scare Stevenson into submission with her mad laughter, but it did. The most harmless of the cops, who was a misfit among his peers, just stood there as a pickup truck with apolitical pro-Indian bumper stickers on it roared up the hill. Emerging was a man in a faded denim jacket and knee-high fringed moccasins. He approached Stevenson first.

"Is he… my eh, ya know… kid all right?" Tom asked.

"Your daughter?" Stevenson replied.

"Which is another issue I don't want to get into now. Her mother doesn't want to or need to, either."

Meanwhile, Leona continued to laugh, cry, and agonize. Her mental focus was alternatively held hostage by a tortured past, an uncertain present, and a gloomy future. She could still hear the conversation around her. She thought it best to let the two men talk and get all the accusations out into the open, each one of them trying to avoid uses of pronouns.

"I don't know what got into… my kid over there, after… my kid over there left," Tom said. "And after enlisting in the Army and getting caught up in wars that my kid never told me or my wife about."

"But sent back a lot of money from after getting into them?" Stevenson proposed. "Maybe your other kid, Paul?"

"I never saw that money," Tom said. "And I didn't want it either."

"Interesting, very interesting," Stevenson said in a small voice, nodding his head as Leona was hitting hers.

"What?" Tom asked. "What's very interesting?"

"That you're more concerned with your daughter… eh… kid's craziness than your mother-in-law's death," the soft-spoken Deputy Sheriff said.

"Huh?" Tom replied.

"Granny," Stevenson explained. "This young woman here kept referring to the older woman as Granny."

"Everyone here calls, or rather called, her Granny," Tom replied with a condescending eye roll.

"Not like your kid over there did," Stevenson replied.

"Granny is not my mother or mother-in-law. And never was!" Tom shot back.

"Does Leona… eh… or Leon know that?"

"Does she have to?"

"No, I suppose not," Stevenson concluded.

With her peripheral hearing, Leona ascertained that Officer Stevenson and her father Tom had a whole lot of secrets that were intriguing and perhaps relevant. She would go digging for what they were later. For now, she still had a very important date to attend and be attentive at.

•••

After a quick change of wardrobe, venue, and strategy, Leona found herself waiting for Boris at a reserved table at the Arrowhead Casino luxury lounge. Though the light was minimal, she could still read the headlines on the Thunder Mountain News Gazette. *Granny Edna Thunder Cloud dies in accidental fire.* Though the wording was a bit different, the photos and the bought and paid for headlines on the Bismarck Country Herald and Big Sky Times were functionally identical. Boris strode over to table, ten minutes late, apologizing for his delay to his dinner guest.

"Good food and good company are worth waiting for," Leona smiled back at him.

Boris saw the way she was looking at the headlines and made a comment on it. "Tragic. I heard you knew her."

Leona put on her best "I don't give a shit" face. It was something she was very good at as Leon when circumstances required it. "Everyone knew her. Or wanted people here to think they did. For a time, anyway. But the old coot is smoking peyote with the Great Spirit now."

"While we become gods and goddesses here," Boris proposed. He asked permission to sit down next to her. She granted it with a goddess-like nod, in keeping with her fabricated station as head of a biological arms and hot-flesh smuggling organization that she had to convince Boris was both real and profitable.

A full-blood Indian teen, barely drinking age, in a skimpy and sexy Pocahontas outfit approached with two menus. Again, by coincidence she was the same as the one who offered her a drink when she was a rich Loonggislandtte housewife on the prowl for a boy-toy. The girl didn't seem to recognize her, but then again, the waitress was having her own problems. Ashley had a glazed look about her eyes, a yellow tinge to the whites of them. Accompanying them were fresh marks on her arms, along with what looked like rope burns on her wrists and neck. But regardless of what she must have experienced, she maintained a bold happy smile on her face.

"What will you be having tonight, Mister

Petrovitch?" she inquired, her voice shaken.

"The usual cocktail to start," Boris smiled back. "And for my associate—"

"Water!" Leona interjected. "No, firewater."

Boris shot a suspicious glance.

"Some temporary liver problems," Leona informed him. "Which are not transmittable," she assured her Russian host. "And besides, madness is best enjoyed straight, and true vision only happens with a clear mind." She turned to the waitress, reading her new nametag. "Right, Running Flower?"

"The customer is always right," the previously alert and spunky Ashley replied, as a very submissive Running Flower with downturned eyes. She adjusted what seemed to be a painful dog collar under her scarf. At Boris's unspoken command, she went to the bar, retrieved two drinks, put them on the table, and then went on her way.

Boris leaned forward in his chair as Leona edged her way forward to read the rest of the menu, and then he poured a portion of his drink into her water glass. "Refusing to drink with a man used to get you killed in the Wild, Wild West. A bullet from a Colt .45 straight to the head," he said while holding his glass.

"Well, this is the new West, with different weapons," Leona answered while still perusing the menu. While doing so, she offered him a private look at the firearms in her oversized but still chic shoulder bag.

He was impressed.

"Yes. It's a variation on an internationally-based theme that isn't supposed to even exist," Leona said regarding the sample at the top of the bag. "More durable, dependable, and reliable than the Tokarev SVTH .38 your father used to push Hitler back to Berlin. And in the hands of whoever will pay top dollar that no one can stop."

Just as Boris reached for the weapon, Leona pulled the bag away. In actuality, it was a replica Carlos made for her from metal pipes and plastic toy guns. Carlos intended it as something Leona could use to scare away fellow Latin American immigrants, who had chosen to join gangs upon entry into the US via Boston. Carlos harbored a special hatred for show-off machismo morons who made their pocket-change stealing pocketbooks from female faculty and students who worked late and went home alone. "I use this little mother's helper for personal protection," Leona said as a fellow addict of the thrill of the kill.

Boris's woody between his legs clearly indicated he was turned on by his dinner companion's anatomy and shared sadistic addictions. "Please tell me more about your affection for the taste of blood," he requested.

Truth be told, Leon had enjoyed the thrill of the kill when working with Boris, and on many occasions, did get a hard-on after he blew the head off of an enemy in the field. But just like Scandinavians in the present who had a vicious Viking past, Leona had outgrown her past. Or had she?

"The blood between my teeth is all my own," she had told her students on many occasions when they got scared of her intensity on the first day of any course she taught. Only a few students understood what she really meant by that. Yet, Leona felt as much personal satisfaction as pity when her scientific competitors got caught fabricating data, sexually assaulting their female grad students, or dipping into their grant money to take their mistresses to Vegas.

"Come on, tell me what parts of your body feels good when you do bad things to other people," Boris asked again, demanding an answer.

Fate intervened, this time, in favor of Leona. Two disgustingly pleasant middle-aged men in plain black suits with neatly combed short hair came into the lounge, waving a warm hello to Boris. Leona took them to be aging Mormon Missionaries who had to repeat their year of fieldwork converting Pagans for the twentieth time. Boris waved a warm hello back to them then to their still hot middle-aged wives who came in to join them. The 40-something Barbies were as domineering as beautiful—it was evident by the way they straightened the ties of their husbands then pulled their view away from younger and perhaps more compliant women who passed by.

"Senator Bill Jackson and Congressman Jack Wilson," Boris whispered to Leona. "Pussy whipped egotists who still think they control all the real money in this state. And as long as we let them think they do, they'll leave us alone while we continue to steal money out of their back pockets. Dumbshit Capitalists."

"Dumbshit capitalists who may not be so innocent or harmless as we think, given their alliances and professional links with these real players," Leona shot back. She scribbled a list of the dangerously influential private companies and military manufacturing contractors on a napkin.

Boris looked over the list of legitimate companies that made their real money doing very illegitimate things, perhaps with or perhaps without the politicians' help. "You seem to know a lot of things about a lot of people," he commented. "And you seem to be a smart and clever woman," he continued, turning his gaze to Leona's poker face.

"That's because I'm a super woman," she replied, never looking up from the menu, perusing the most expensive items. "Who needs to work with a Superman so business is not so… hmmm…"

"Boring?" Boris offered.

"Da, Comrade," she smiled back.

"But I am particularly interested in the kind of weapons you have that are more biological than mechanical," the Russian KGB snarled. "With safeguards built into them so if any of our people get exposed, they will be protected or cured, of course. It's something few business partners I've had were able to deliver."

"Which I can deliver," Leona affirmed, putting down the menu. She looked into Boris' eyes, holding them hostage with an intense stare. He still did not recognize her, nor picked up on the fact she was bluffing more than she ever had in her life. "Yes, I can deliver to you anything you need or want."

"I will need proof. As a scientist in the service of... us, I think you will understand."

"That I do. But there is one rule of biology that the idiots like the ones who obey all the rules and assholes like us who make them—must obey."

"Above all else, do no harm to the people you are working for?" Boris proposed.

Leona laughed at his joke, as such was expected of her both as a woman and a new partner. Once Boris's ego was satiated, she went on to explain her point in plainer English. "If we don't eat, we can't think effectively. So it stands to reason that if we eat well, we think very effectively."

"Which means you will indeed have the most

expensive items on the menu?" he asked.

"It's my duty to do so, and your pleasure to enjoy me doing it. Is that not so?" she replied with a warm upturning of her ruby red lips.

"Yes, it is so," he said, chuckling with appreciative pleasure at her pun, for now anyway.

CHAPTER 9

"I need three more hours before I'll be free. Send your driver for me, then." She pressed the end call button on her phone. Leona had no choice but to delay the next meeting with Boris. To keep up her persona of an arms dealer, she would need more biological weapons and guns. She had to figure how to get all the supplies, and she'd already drained her emergency savings and paid for the present accommodations with a credit card bearing someone else's name. She'd gone back on the promise she'd made to herself, and swore she would not pay for needs or wants with fake or stolen credit cards like her past self had. But the present owner of this card was a rich bitch real estate mogul who made her fortune turning hard working stiffs into homeless bums. There was one thing Leona could not buy using M. C. Horowitz's overstocked overseas bank—time.

She had no idea how long she had before the owner would become aware of the transactions, and it concerned her. She had to act fast but had no choice except to wait for the package from Carlos. She looked at her watch, noting the time.

"Carlos could have driven here with the package of biological goodies I need faster than the courier I overpaid," she said, watching the cockroach scurry across the floor. She threw him another chunk of the filet mignon sent to her as a complimentary perk from the front desk. “You don’t seem to be choking on it or spacing out with your legs in the air, so that means that the hotel manager, who I think really does have the hots for me, didn’t deliver me a steak spiced with deadly hemlock gravy. Or some kind of truth serum that will make me say, for maybe the first time, what’s on my mind without censoring it. That would make more sense if Boris is still threatened by me or testing me. What are your opinions on that, Fred, or is it Fredericka? But the main question here is…” she asked the cockroach as it continued to dine without any ill effects.

She heard a rumbling in her belly just before she felt the hunger pangs. It reminded her of the eight day extraction of civilian prisoners missions overseas as Leon when she was without food for days. Common sense and hard experience told her the brain does need some food to stay fresh, alert, and alive. Still, she insisted on fasting so she could obtain the needed spiritual insight. It was a noble endeavor, but she was faced with a favorite meal, and the aroma made it hard to resist.

Leona’s never-resting brain focused on the latest toxins she’d developed to simulate naturally occurring neurological diseases which would help her come up with a cure. The recipients of those toxins were rats in her lab, who were also the test subjects for potential cures. Fred, or Fredericka, reminded her of those rodents for which she really did develop feelings, despite the cruel things she had to do to them in order to meet her goal.

"Yeah, I suppose I was a necessary evil in the lab also," she said to the roach as she finally gave in to temptation by taking a small bite of the steak. While doing so, she offered a larger portion to her six-legged diner companion. "You're brave to come out in the light like this, unlike your other comrades who are probably still hiding behind the wall somewhere in the dark, Fred or Fredericka. Either that or you're just plain stupid or you have a death wish to be squashed."

She thought about going on the Internet to read the roach a chapter or two from *Metamorphosis* by Kafka, an insightful but depressive tale about a man who wakes up as a Cockroach and has to deal with it.

"Hey, maybe you're my Prince Charming who will turn into the man who will accept me as a real woman if I kiss you on the lips, or maybe your ass," she mused. "But then again, I suppose we have to stay on more formal terms as you're possibly my Spirit Messenger, sent by Granny from the Huya Aniya. Or maybe, you're Granny, returned from the dead to..."

Leona's indulgence in fantasy was interrupted by a knock on the door. Arming herself with Carlos' fake gun, she looked through the peephole. "Package for Maria C. Horowitz," a man in a ball cap covering his face said. “A heavy one.”

Leona opened the door, paid the courier with a large tip, and then dismissed him. Once he was gone, she looked inside the package. Carlos had sent everything she needed for the next stage of the mission. Amongst the chemicals, armaments, and medical equipment was a greeting card from Rachel thanking Leona for pulling her out of “the abyss of academic comfort.” Rachel wrote further that she demanded to “be put into the front lines of whatever war you’re about to start, ASAP.”

“When the time is right, I’ll bring you into all of this,” Leona texted Rachel back. “Right now, I need you there to look after home cave,” she continued typing, thinking for the first time that she would never see home cave in Massachusetts U ever again. Given what Leona would be doing with Boris in less than three hours, such was a very real possibility.

Boris’ private car picked Leona up at the prescribed time. She was driven to the new hospital on the Rez, which bore his name as the primary funder. Two of Boris’ most well-dressed and well-armed bodyguards escorted her past the moderately populated general admission lobby to a well equipped yet under populated ER, and then to a darkened under construction hallway leading to the Psych Ward.

In Room 203, the patient lay quiet, her eyes fixed on the ceiling. Around her wrists and ankles were the latest in psych patient restrains, meant to be strong enough to hold her down but soft enough to prevent leaving marks if she struggled. The first thing Leona noticed when she sized up the woman was a leather-fringed Indian maiden necklace around her neck stained with dried blood and fecal matter.

Holding the device that activated the electrocuting unit attached to the necklace was one of Boris' senior goons with sadistic eyes. Two young enforcers, who were more obedient than passionate, stood by in white lab coats and rubber gloves on their dirty, grubby bloodstained hands.

Leona watched it all from the one-way mirror dividing Room 203.

Boris by her side in the observation chamber said, "Sometimes training people to do what is in their best interest is easy. Sometimes it is harder." He pressed a button on the wall, causing the light inside the room to acquire a reddish hue.

The senior goon nodded the younger ones to proceed. The two younger men took off their lab coats and commenced to have their way with Maria, with ample male anatomical parts at the ready to do so.

"Smile, Maria," the older goon requested of the patient.

"I'm not Maria!" she persisted in resisting the affection being shown to her despite the fact she was electrocuted each time she did. Having nothing to lose, she bit into the closest, causing them to back off for the moment anyway. In the struggle, the senior doctor fell backward, making it hard to elevate the intensity of the jolts. While being shocked, the young woman yelled out to the mirror. "I'm not Maria Beaver Mouth! Or Maria 3. I am Eva Anna Rodriguez, from—"

Her desperate attempt to reach anyone beyond the mirror was put to a halt when the enraged senior goon upped the electrocution to maximal strength. Boris shut down the power on his electrocution devise and commanded through the microphone leading to a loudspeaker to lower in a language Leona did not understand. From the reaction of the doctor and the dosage lowering, she knew it was to keep Eva's suffering, sparing her the merciful end of a jolt that would fry her brain into a burnt crisp.

It made Leona sick to stand and watch the young woman being tortured, but she had to remain focused on the end result. She knew if Boris discovered her real identity, it would ruin everything. She recalled how Boris reacted in the Arab village they destroyed in an attempt to save it; he killed all within his path.

The head goon behind the one-way mirror went into a tantrum, demanding he be put in charge of the young woman's training. At Boris's command from the other side of the mirror, he was relieved of duty by the next in line, who punched his former superior into the mouth then the gut. A fight ensued between the old goon and his former subordinate. The third goon in the room was instructed via his ear bud from Boris not to interfere with the game.

Meanwhile, Boris remained cool and collected, his hands lacking any blood from any of victims on the other side of the mirror. *That's Boris, all right*, Leona thought, recalling the good old days as Leon. *Keeping tortured prisoners alive as long as possible so he could enjoy seeing them in pain. While he gets off on the thrill of pitting everyone under him against each other so they could rise up the ladder to attain the pleasure of being his favorite lap dog and best buddy. Like I did, God help me.*

As for that Almighty, Boris did have a relationship with such, just like his patron saint Comrade Stalin. Just like that infamous man of steel he considered every action he did as being justified because it was in service of his World Vision. Both Stalin and Boris considered themselves to be in competition with God, while at the same time denying His existence to anyone in public and fearing him in private. Such was what Leona was honored to see in the past and horrified to observe again in the present.

Just as God created Adam et al to alleviate his loneliness, Boris needed companions to rule the world with him. Leon was once one of those trusted companions. Leona now had to take over that place without being noticed.

Leona fantasized about getting Boris alone, putting a dog collar on him, and frying his brains out until there was no life in his body. It would be contra-indicated, as he was no doubt connected to a network of other Boris's who trafficked weapons, sex slaves, and God knows what else. She was not only nabbing bad-fish Boris but every toxic creature swimming in the ocean. Of course, such a noble task required one heroic victory at a time, without incurring collateral damage on any tortured minnows.

"Maria 3, otherwise known as Maria Beaver Mouth, Leona," Boris said, admiring the defective comfort woman behind the one-way mirror with still defiant eyes that seemed to follow his. "It is hard to say if she's giving that vengeful stare at herself in the mirror or if it is to whomever she is imagining is behind it. In any case, she is a suitable model for the medications you say will turn an angry, thinking, assertive bitch into a happy, dumb, and obedient puppy dog. I trust your special medications will make involuntarily obedient people into voluntarily happy ones, my dear, Leona. It is ineffective business to fry the life out of specimens who can potentially service my many clients. I do hope you can provide me with new ways to make people compliant, happy, and obedient."

"You mean like country music and Top Forty pabulum muzac which woes free thinking listeners into head-boppers?" Leona offered, easing into unapologetically satirical hillbilly diction. "Then makes toe tappers and clap-along crowds do whatever the master says at their factory jobs on Monday morning? All the songs with three chords and no more than twice as many lyrics that make it fun to be dumb? Not like the complicated music of Wolfgang-me-with-a-spoon Mozart, Rickie Wagner, and Jimbo Shitsokovitch that makes your head hurt because if forces you to think. Which, if ya ain't careful, can lead to, yeah, you got it, readin'."

Boris smiled at her jokes and cultural digs. She found herself finally finding some common cultural ground with the Harvard and University of Moscow educated Russian businessman. That ground gave way to a shaky foundation when he pointed to the bag of biological tricks in her briefcase. "Is there anything you will need from us for your demonstration, Doctor Leona, whose surname I don't know and have stopped caring about?"

"To be alone with her as I give her the treatment for defiant rage syndrome, category 3 according to my classification of it by the looks of this guinea pig," Leona replied.

"Of course, with the appropriate precautions," he answered. Boris took Leona's hand into his then stroked her manicured fingers, which thankfully were not excessively large for her new gender.

Leona was not sure if precaution meant being sure the young woman didn't bite off her fingers or that Boris wanted to see who Leona really was. In any case, the audition of Leona's special biological agent that could convert mass numbers of freethinking citizens of a disobedient country into passive, happy slaves was on.

Boris yelled some commands Leona didn't recognize into the ear buds of the two warring goons, who ceased hostilities, and on his second request, shook hands. He then allowed her to enter the treatment room by herself. *Maybe that charming bastard really does trust me,* she thought as she put on a professional-looking lab coat at the door to the other portion of room 206. She preceded to the joy of the patient, who had learned to bite into the digits of those who tried to teach her acceptable manners. *Or maybe because Comrade Boris ran out of assistants with even tempers and intact fingers,* she considered through a well-needed self-administered chuckle. But whatever the reason, the key question here was whether Maria 3 would trust her.

By the expressions spewing out of her, she didn't. Leona recognized some of the Spanish curses delivered between the spits she directed at her face. Anticipating what the gentleman mobster would retaliate on the woman or have his goons do it, Leona held her hand up to Boris on the other side of the mirror. "I'm all right and have to go through with this" she conveyed to him in gesture and words. She then requested Boris empty the room of the now-calmed down goons assigned to protect her. After what felt like a tense delay from the other end, he complied.

While the spit and curse fest continued, Leona set about retrieving the appropriate biological goodies. She remained silent while loading a syringe with a carefully dispensed proportion of coded solutions A, B, and C. But she did have to say something when woman unleashed an insult to her in very correctly pronounced Cree.

"That curse, insult, and prediction means..." she replied, feeling the impact of the words tearing into her heart.

"Die in hell, you sick bitch," the apparently half-Indian, half-Mexican problem patient spat back at her in English.

"More accurately, die in hell, you necessary evil," Leona replied softly in her best Cree then in what she hoped was passable Spanish, praying the microphones above her didn't pick it up. "Do a little harm now to do a lot of good later," she whispered in a mixture of the two languages that woman seemed to both hear and understand. “A mathematical calculation, which will go much easier for you if you—”

“—just fucking relax!?” she shot back, expecting the worst as Leona edged the syringe toward her mouth.

“Yes, please, just relax,” Leona replied with dispassionate professional affirmation, posing for the cameras and no doubt the horny packed house at the other side of the one-way mirror watching her. “This syringe under the tongue, now,” she commanded as a dominatrix, appended by a light kick into Maria C’s belly with her pointed boots made to look hard by pushing her head downward into a bowed position.

Leona’s sensitive hearing could detect the cheers of the Wolf Pack from the other side of the one-way see-through mirror. Her fingers felt the tension in the woman’s body ease up. “Drink everything that’s in this syringe now,” she ordered her in English.

“And this for later, when you are alone, Eva,” Leona appended softly in Cree. She gently pulled out a wrapped pill from inside her shirt and instructed her to take it in thirty minutes—indicated by six shows of five fingers and a discrete pointing at her watch. That very private patient doctor session was all out of view of any cameras, so Leona hoped anyway.

Leona then retrieved a key from the hidden recesses of her lab coat pocket. It did indeed fit into the lock in Maria C’s dog collar. “It’s up to you to take it off, Eva, use it only when the time is right," Leona whispered into her ear.

"Yes, that's my name, Eva," she slurred out from her parched lips through a badly bruised jaw, staring vacantly into space.

"Eva is your name," Leona replied as she slipped the key into Maria 3's bruised and bloodied vulva, attaching it to the baggie containing the pills. "Pretend this is what the assholes out there out there think it is," she whispered, as she placed the syringe containing the official obedience cocktail into Eva's mouth. "Under the tongue," she continued. "Pretend that it turns you into the voluntarily obedient slave that we both know you aren't. It is going to make you a bit drowsy, but as soon as you feel it, take that reversal agent I put into the your still very private parts. It'll give you the strength and know how to overpower these shitheads."

Eva raised her tongue and allowed Leona to squeeze a bolus of one-part super-diluted real sedative and ninety-nine percent real hyper-concentrated Kool-Aid into her mouth.

"Now," Dominatrix-Scientist Leona said loudly, sensing curious and watchful eyes on the other side of the mirror. "I want you to smile for me and mean it."

Maybe it was the specific command given to smile, or the spot in Eva's vulva that had been touched, or a combination of the two. Eva's Post-Traumatic-Stress-

Syndrome buttons had been pushed. She turned into a raging animal, somehow getting loose from her restraints; she grabbed hold of Leona's long black hair, turning her neck briskly to the right then smashing her head to the floor. Eva grabbed hold of the sharpest scalpel in Leona's kit, about to slit her throat. Before it could cut open her carotid artery, a bullet from an open door pierced her dead.

Leona had enough presence of mind to grab hold of the reversal agent and the stolen master key to the bitch collar attached to it. She quickly inserted them into the panties under her dress with her right hand, while examining her patient with her left. Though there was large hole in Eva's cranium revealing pulsating brain tissue, only a small amount of blood flowed out of it.

"Specially-designed bullet," Boris explained by way of explanation as he strolled into the room proudly holding the smoking gun. "Leaves no mess afterward… perhaps we can design a bullet that leaves no bleeding afterward." He dipped his finger into the hole in Eva's head then pulled it out it to examine how much blood was on it. He extended his tongue for a taste of freshly bullet-fried brains. "Still messy blood on this bullet. But I'm sure you and the scientist working for you can devise cleaner, less traceable, and deadlier Ammo than us." He offered Leona a taste of fresh blood.

"Gave it up for Lent." She cringed, scaring herself at

how well the mask of being cold and cruel fit around a heart that was horrified and hurting. "Besides, scientists are not supposed to eat their lab rats. A rule we somehow obey. But this lab rat… she seems, or rather seemed, interesting."

"That and valuable," Boris replied with a fond and nostalgic grimace. "We conscripted her for very high paying clients. But soon afterward, we discovered she had biological problems. Maybe too many drugs she took before we liberated her from a life of mainstream morality or the ones some of my handlers used to keep her hand-able. Even I can't supervise the medications all of my employees or what they do with their property," he lamented. "It might be why your medications didn't work the way you expected it to?"

"Most probably," Leona replied, doing her best to keep her heart cold and her mind thinking.

"But we need less dangerous specimens," Boris added as he helped Leona up from the floor.

"Thanks, I owe you one," Leona replied with a lilt in her voice.

"Yes, you do."

CHAPTER 10

It wasn't what Leona saw when she entered the dormitory but what she smelled in the room housing the specimens to be experimented with or sold to the highest bidder. Each was branded with a bar code and kept in line with a collar around their neck. Rushing into her nose was the stench of love juices, feces, urine, and blood, all connected by the aromas of terror and hopelessness. The young women ranged from the tender age of twelve to the ripe old seasoned age of thirty-five. Most of them were emaciated, though in an alluring sort of way. Some were allowed or medically altered to be plump in portions of their anatomy areas. Their skin pigmentations were white, black, red, and yellow. Their hair, for the most part, was long, alluring, and well kept, despite the fact they were probably not allowed to wash themselves. From what she could tell, they were not allowed to do anything except remain chained to their beds to cry themselves to sleep, eat whatever rations they were allowed, and avail themselves of a variety of addictive pharmaceuticals to either numb their pain or to maintain a buzz between their ears.

Amanda 21 and Jacque 3 shot themselves up with dope. Rainbow 2 and Carla 5 were having the happy juice given to them by a medic who, ominously, looked a lot like Leona would have at this point in life had she remained as Leon.

"The usual accommodations," Boris commented to her regarding what was inside the closed, condemned, and now windowless building that had been the old Rez Recreational Center. "They like this time of day. Feeding and medication time."

Another woman was dragged into the room still struggling. She was Yolanda 2 according to the new employee number on her collar. Though she was gagged, she still managed to grunt out her accusations and anger. They were quickly quenched when one of Boris' medical goons shot a syringe full of a coded medication into her arm. Before giving in to the happy juice, Yolanda extended third fuck you finger. After the elixir found its way into her brain, that digit turned flaccid, followed by tremors in all of her extremities for ten horrifying seconds, after which her entire body went limp.

It made her sick to stand and watch the abuse inflicted upon them, but there was nothing she could do. She lowered her gaze to get a better look at the women without being noticed, but none of them looked back at her. Some kept their eyes downward when she looked in their direction because they were lost in a world the addictive medication provided.

Others turned away because they were instructed by their caretakers to keep their heads down in the presence of any unapproved strangers. But Yolanda 2 looked up at Leona before fading into being someone else.

"Help me," she mouthed as her eyes closed halfway and faded into semi-consciousness.

Before Leona could give her an answer with her mouth, or eyes, Boris returned to her side with a stack of medical files. "Take a look at them," he said. "See which ones are most suitable for experimentation with those drugs you say makes obedient people happy as well. Happy is far better for business than submissive, or high, after all."

"Yes, indeed," Leona replied, pretending to be well versed in the management and sales of such human merchandise as she glanced over the files. She remembered when Leon traded human beings for valuable intel with regard to the Mission at hand, once those humans were dehumanized of course. It was something he was well experienced in, as the most effective soldier is one who can dehumanize his enemy and enjoy the thrill of dominating him. It was that primal hunting instinct that predator needed in order to act quickly and rapidly enough to neutralize prey and not become the prey.

Boris was handed more medical charts for all of the women by a well-armed orderly. He glanced at them then handed them over to Leona. "Their current medical evaluations, blood work, psychological proclivities, and cultural backgrounds. I took the liberty of gathering all the information you would need on them so you could make them into what we will need, between the ears and below the neck," he related with pride accompanied by an aristocratic bow.

The information was thorough and not only medically. They included the origin of the girls prior to their abduction, their known history as once-free souls. Each graded from 1-10 on how easy it would be to re-educate and become a marketable slave. Boris was always a thorough military leader who prided himself on knowing as much as he could about his friends, enemies, and prisoners. On more than one occasion he claimed the effectiveness of the Soviet Gulag system could have been far greatly improved if Russian record keeping matched the level of completeness and sophistication of the Nazis. Then again, combining the most sadistic elements of Joseph Stalin with the mass-pleasing charisma of Adolf Hitler was something Boris always did so well. Such was one reason why he was a first round pick to be hired by private companies interested in protecting their economic interests or clandestine government agencies that worked with them.

Leona didn't know exactly why Boris was now in business for himself but such was inevitable. Digging in her memory, she recalled Boris boasted to her former self as Leon that he was smarter than his employers, and that after milking the cows dry he would butcher them and dine on their most tender flesh.

During all of those lucrative, colorful, and dangerous days as a mercenary, Leon was not only Boris's favorite protégée but also his only trusted friend. Such was what Leona recalled yet again as she found herself fading away into shouldas and couldas land behind her eyes, while trying to look like she was assessing which of the five rows of girls chained to iron cots would be most suitable for her psycho-active drug trials.

"Is there something wrong?" Boris asked her, in a gentlemanly manner, reading her soul as well as her mind.

"No, nothing. All is in order," she answered with a cold, insensitive voice, as her heart recalled the history of how these women got there.

They were stories like Meeta's. She was a barefoot thirteen-year-old dirt-poor East Indian girl returning home after getting an A in her reading assignments in school. She felt proud while telling her father the teacher wanted to promote her to the next grade ahead of schedule. Her father smiled with sorrow at the news, as he had already made arrangements to have her schooled by a non-blood-related uncle from Australia who needed an additional mistress for himself and play-toy for his clients. Meeta's mother begged her husband to not let Uncle Jim take Meeta away, but she also knew that the sale of her daughter would enable her other ten children to eat for the year and perhaps two.

Then there were the stories of two Albanian girls arriving in Italy on a private yacht after winning a talent and modeling contest back home. Trina and Mileva were not greeted by an executive from MGM studios who would be their acting coach. Instead, an ugly over-the-hill Madame who instructed one of her associates to take the passports from the two sixteen-year-old Albanians and then had them whisked away into a black limo with shaded windows. Trina's parents made inquiries about where their daughter were. The Milanese Police told them her body was burned in a traffic accident. Mileva's brother made inquiries into the whereabouts of his day-dreaming sister, a noble act for which he was rewarded by being cut up by the Albanian mob and fed to the pigs.

Some of Boris's conscripted and unpaid employees were from Leona's own country. One example was Sophie DeAngelo, an honor student from Englewood, New Jersey, who was given special permission by her mom to celebrate her eighteenth birthday in Manhattan with her best friend who'd just moved to Soho. The hot looking brunette who'd never let a horny boy into her pants despite the rumors in the boys' locker room, danced the night away in the Big Apple till closing time. Sophie restricted herself to having only one beer so she would not get pulled over by the cops for a DWI on her way back to Jersey. After saying goodnight to her best girlfriend and to her perhaps first worthwhile new Manhattanite boyfriend, Sophie walked happily alone amongst a few other late night stragglers. Half a block from the parking spot she was lucky enough to get six hours earlier, Sophie was pulled into an alley and forced into a car and driven to the airport where a private jet destined for the Cayman Islands awaited.

The girls who grew up in the Bible belt were not spared either. Rebecca von Klept was a blonde, blue-eyed Amish girl who finally reached her sixteenth birthday and was eligible for Rumspringa, which encouraged her to experiment and explore the world for a year before returning home to commit herself to the Community and the Lord. She was a very good pianist but wanted to become an excellent one so she could play for the Community, the Lord, and to a room full of her own children someday who would also praise the Almighty in music and song.

An opportunity to study at Julliard opened up courtesy of a Lincoln Center executive and his female companion who got lost on their way to Ithaca, accidently heard Rebecca's musical interpretation of Bach's *Jesu, Joy of Man's Desiring*. As Rebecca's two twin brothers were close enough to eighteen, her father insisted they tag along with their younger sister, staying in the Big Apple as long as they wanted or needed to.

Rebecca stepped off the bus at the Port Authority in New York, where she took a cab to her father's ex-Amish brother's house in Queens. Unlike her brothers, she was still in her traditional Amish attire, intending to clad herself into worldly clothes after settling in at a safe destination.

Around her were more people than she had ever seen in such a small place. All expressed their frustrations, joys, and opinions about the world very loudly. She smiled as she listened but soon laughed when she saw her two brothers proudly taking photos of each other with the Chinese exchange students they met on the bus with their new pocket cameras. A baggage handler offered to help Rebecca with her luggage. He said his brother had just bought his own cab, that he could use to take her and whoever she wanted anywhere in the city for half price. Rebecca asked her brothers if they wanted to join her, but they declined, saying they would catch up to her at Uncle Fritz's in a few hours. Rebecca never arrived at Uncle Fritz's house. After a frustrating two weeks dealing with the NYPD, her brothers went back home to the farm as failures to themselves and disappointments to their family.

"Thirty million more of them around the world," Leona said to herself regarding the other missing girls, women and young boys living as sex slaves, as according to the most conservative statistics. "And that's probably the tip of the iceberg."

"Iceberg?" Boris inquired, having heard her.

"For dinner, tonight," Leona replied. "Iceberg lettuce. And some steak, potatoes, and fresh vegetables."

"I know just the place," Boris informed her.

"Which is right here. I can't experiment with specimens that aren't well nourished, no matter how normal their blood-work and physical exam sheets say they are. Any rancher out here knows well-fed cattle always bring in the best prices."

"Yes," Boris acknowledged. "But the extra expenses will come out of your cut of the profits."

"Profits that will be very large indeed if we work together," she replied. Seeing the need to up the ante, she continued, gently stroking Boris's cheek with her tender fingers. "And play together once the work is done?"

Boris said "yes" with his eyes to her unspoken terms. The thought of going to bed with such a manifestation of evil horrified Leona, but the continued promise to do so would buy her badly needed time. While her brain strategized over what to do next with Boris, her mind assessed what had happened to her soul since her arrival.

She had initially left her new life in comfortable academia and come to the Rez to investigate the death of her brother. He was family. She escalated her efforts to see that justice was served after Granny was killed. She was family, too. And now, all of the slaves under Boris's thumb were also family, as were the estimated thirty million other owned pieces of human merchandise being held someplace in the world by another Boris's.

What was left of Leona's biological family was useless, but perhaps she was mistaken about that. Thinking quick, she purposely slipped on the floor so she could insert a high-powered mini-microphone on the wall next to the dormitory administrative office.

CHAPTER 11

"Do you understand all that Russian?" Leona's father asked.

Leona moved closer to the static-producing computer to hear what was coming out of the rebuilt microphones Carlos has originally made for her to spy on her academic rivals, but she had refused to use them. Perhaps her refusal to listen on her academic rivals and comrades was honorable. Or maybe she was afraid of finding out that her hard-earned friends were really just temporary allies, vicious predators, or undiscovered parasites.

"Whatever they're saying, it sounds nasty and cruel," the co-listener interjected regarding the conversation from the administration room in the slaves' dormitory just as he sensed Leona getting lost in the past again.

"And cool to those with power and influence, Dad," Leona said to Tom.

He nodded and upped the volume while fussing with a few wires in the back of the mismatched speakers to make them behave well. A skill he'd learned when doing sound checks for rock concerts, powwows, and power-to-our-people political rallies back in the sixties. Whatever he did worked; the words were clear. However, the subtext of the conversations Boris was having with his subordinates and his collaborators was dark as a moonless night.

"I can understand most of the Russian and some of the Albanian, but to be sure of what we have, we'll need a translator," Leona said. "As for the Chinese and most of the Arabic, that's all Greek to me."

Tom couldn't understand what was being said, but one word frightened the crap out of him, particularly when Boris said it. "Leona." The tone in the other voices warned him the men speaking were dangerous, and that scared him not only for his safety but also Leona's. Seeing he accidently left one of the windows partially open, he got up, and closed it. Then he readjusted the blinds on the each of the windows, being sure absolutely no light could come in through them. He didn't want to take any chances of someone spying on them.

"Leona, Boris keeps referring to you with a scary agenda."

"But a respected title," Leona replied. "Doctor Leona."

"And he still doesn't know your last name?"

"Only from all those research papers I published, which are public record, Dad. And which I changed when I went to college to get a biology degree after mastering the death sciences as Leon," she explained regarding her dropping the surname she was given at birth. "Besides, I told Boris that my academic life, in a location he never asked about, is over. And that when it existed, it was a cover."

"A cover that's a very big accomplishment, Doctor Leona," Tom said, still not used to addressing his oldest and what he thought was most responsible, establishment, and manly offspring. "Particularly because of where our family came from."

Tom treated himself to yet another look at the photos of himself, his wife, and his two sons during the good old days in front of the converted school bus they called home when they were rich in vision, affluent in defiance, and broke in pocket. His eyes were focused on the name that followed the 'L' on the copies of Leona's B.S. and Ph.D. diplomas prominently placed above the rest of the family photos.

"Boris knows you as Doctor Zimmerman," he commented, bitterness simmering in his tone.

"But not the name I grew up with, here and with him," she said. "I had to buy a new identity to earn a legitimate life as a scientist, teacher, and whatever else I've become after leaving behind everything and everyone here. It was for everyone's good."

"But Chief Boris or whatever his real name is, will figure out you have a legitimate job as a research scientist and college lecturer," Tom warned.

"It is completely consistent with it." Leona assured her father with a gentle hand on his shaking yet muscular shoulder. "As I told Boris, academic people have lots of time to themselves, take lots of trips, and only have to check in to their posts to spout out bullshit to easily fool students at the lectern for thirty hours a year. To please their chairman, they go to a few fundraisers. When they have to keep up with their publication quota, they fake some data or their own twice a year. Or they repeat a great study done by another lab after they give it a rotten review so it doesn't get published by the people who did it in the first place. Or they test the latest most toxic chemicals known to man or beast and somehow find them to have no deleterious effects on lab animals so the manufacturers can inflict them on the human public, with, of course, a healthy grant to the scientist who did the independent testing—"

"And all of that in plain English is...?" Tom interjected in an accusative tone.

"What I don't do and never did!" Leona replied.

"Yes, I know." He seemed to believe Leona, yet his mind still wasn't ready to accept all the changes. He'd been overloaded with way too many soul-awakening insights in a brief period of time. One of those insights dealt with Granny and the ledger Leona had placed in front of him several realizations ago. Finally, he picked it up, reluctant to open it. "Do I want to know what's in there, Leona?"

"The truth shall set you free, Dad."

"Or get you killed."

"It's always a good day to die," Leona reminded him in Cree. "Isn't that the battle cry Granny always told us? And isn't that also the battle cries you used to say to yourself and others when you fought against the Palefaces as an Indian Liberation Organizer?"

Tom considered the dare then took it. He opened the ledger, examining it with a critical and cynical eye. Most of the details seemed to baffle him, but what he could make of it, made him green in the gills and apparently sick to his stomach.

"Numbers, figures, conversational transcripts, and dates that are incriminating to a lot of people we know and more powerful people we don't know yet, anyway," Leona said by way of summary. "From someone who was once the most respected bookkeeper and personal counselor on this Rez and five others around it. Dirty laundry on lots of *clean* people."

"Who are not so clean now, by the looks of this. But, in a court of law, or a cop's interrogation room, no one would believe it." He closed the book and handed it back to her. "No one would believe it. Even I wouldn't believe it if I was assigned the job of being the judge. We all loved Granny, but she made up and believed stories about animals who talked to her in the woods. She could have made up stories about these financial figures and business transactions as well and used her bookkeeping skills, she could have made them look balanced, and legal. It's all, as they say on those cop shows which are not reality, speculation."

"Like the speculation that Paul died of natural causes? He was rising up high in Chief Boris's casino till his job and life were terminally ended. That is fact, not speculation."

Tom didn't seem to have either the courage to affirm Leona's conviction or the stomach to keep denying it.

"Come on, Dad," she pleaded. She put her hand on Tom's shoulder in the same manner that he did for her when she was a kid who needed assurance as well as courage. "I don't believe the official Medical Examiner's report any more than you do."

Tom thought long and hard. Finally, he gave voice to his most effective suggestion regarding the dilemma. "Sheriff Stevenson."

"Deputy lap dog Stevenson?" Leona mused, as disappointed in the man as she was angered at him.

"What does he know about all of this?" Tom asked, demanding a direct, black and white answer.

"That he'll keep investigating it," Leona said, angrily staring into space regarding the last conversation she had with the deputy over the phone on what he said was his private line. "In his spare time, of course. While he gets paid by the Band Council to not investigate anything of course." After vicariously condemning Stevenson to the special circle of hell designed for those who commit the eighth primal sin of being overly cautious, she turned to Tom. "Look, Dad. At one time, you and Mom wanted to change the world. Merge the American Indian Movement with the Woodstock Flower Power People's Revolution. I know that AIM sold out to the man after Disco came into power, and that the only power left in the People's Revolution was in their ability sell t-shirts to mall rats who think Woodstock is a Swedish brand of upscale furniture. But this Revolution here and now! The chance to be alive and free again is up to us!"

"More like it's up to you," Tom replied after a pensive pause. His wrinkled tired face said the rest. He pushed back his long black hair. It had turned far grayer than Leona had ever noticed and with what looked like a Paleface bald spot developing on the crown.

Leona felt disappointed then powerless.

"You can do it," Tom assured her with his hand on her shoulder. "You used to be a cop in a city loaded with crime, remember? A man's man. An Injun and a white man's man?"

"Until the night I went undercover as a woman. An assignment I didn't want to do. But as soon as the dress met my legs and my feet slipped into those heels," Leona said, recalling the internal and external events of that very eventful day.

"You found out that you liked it?" Tom offered.

"That I always liked it. Ever since I was seven. And needed to do it to be me. To be complete. Like the manly Army commercials said, to 'be all you can be'." Leona released the sorrow, pain, and anguish of those times into ironic laughter.

"You could have told me, Leona."

"And you would have understood it?" She held back tears of regret as she faced the only man she ever loved in the truest sense of the word. "Or tried to accept it, Dad? I asked you once, I think it was at a powwow, when I think I was nine, as a joke, what you would do if I came to the powwow, or to a basketball game, or to school wearing a dress. You said, without any humor at all in your voice, 'I'll kill ya'."

"Maybe I would have then, but now…"

A special moment was in the works for Tom and Leona. They looked into each other's eyes. After daring to not deny what they saw, father and son-turned-daughter edged toward each other in an embrace that eased all of the pain. It redeemed all of the suffering they had endured since she left the Rez so long ago. But the universe had a different idea.

"Happy birthday to you," her mother said, clad in a white woman's dress with a very large Christian cross around her neck. She shuffled into the room with a gait more befitting a frumpy *Everyone Loves Raymond* grandmother than the freewheeling, musically-rebellious hippie mom she once was. “Happy Birthday, dear Leon,” she continued, pushing a birthday cake addressing Leona as Leon in front of her, thirty-eight candles all lit and ready to blow out. Then she insisted Tom join her repeating that lyric exactly as she had sung it.

“Happy birthday to you,” Tom sang along with Emily, closing up his heart and spirit again.

“Blow out the candles, Leon,” Emily insisted.

Leona looked to Tom as to what to do next. He replied with a “your mother is one of them, not us” nod of his head when Emily wasn’t looking.

Leona had no choice but to blow out the candles then say “thank you” to Emily. Her once politically savvy and open soul mother had grown into the kind of woman who couldn’t handle the truth. Leona was now dedicated to the truth more than ever.

CHAPTER 12

Deputy Sheriff Stevenson sat in his secluded office looking up at his Canadian Grandfather's more-stain-than-shine hunting knife. Next to it hung the moccasins his grandmother had worn down to nothing on the soles while waiting for her husband to come home from excursions in the bush. His desk was overloaded with case files and incomplete paperwork on the left-hand side. On the other side sat memos from the brass warning him that the parking tickets, building code violations, and complaints about excess noise needed to be dealt with quickly or the desk and him would be removed from the building permanently.

Laughing off the thought of them boxing up years of service, he turned his focus to Granny's ledger and the sound bites selected from the recordings obtained from the slave dormitory.

Leona anxiously awaited, hoping he was not on Boris's payroll and would help. She didn't know who else to turn to, and after spying on him for the past week, she believed he was clueless to all the happenings. Tom strongly advised that to gain the cooperation of the least corrupt and possibly trustable cop on the Rez, she had to let him in on her biological secrets and cultural origins.

"How many people on the Rez know about you being a… ya know… a—" Stevenson asked.

"Human being?" Leona shot back. "Who wants to get the shitheads listed in that ledger and recorded in the dormitory office out of our lives here so we can get back to the crappy lives we used to live before we got affluent?"

Stevenson removed the earplugs connected to the tape player then put down the ledger. He took gentle hold of an old, weather-beaten bridle made of moose-hide and horsehair hanging on the very private museum wall behind him.

"Our lives then were not that crappy," he said with a fond smile, recalling memories Leona felt she could relate to very well. "I remember riding my horse to work when the weather was good."

"And snowshoeing when the weather was bad," Leona added, her gaze captured by the artistry and history of a pair of snowshoes besides the bridle.

"Buying and selling firewater was illegal on the Rez then," he recalled with the nostalgia of an eighty-something old fart rather than a forty-something work-still-in-progress. "Most people followed that law at the general store. Some even honored it at home."

"Yeah, honor," Leona pushed through a hushed sigh. Seeing that Stevenson was lost in the world of the past, she pushed the ledger and associated notes back into his hands so he could deal with the present.

Stevenson looked at them again, still seeming very

casual about it all. One of the photos within the notes featured Boris in full Native headdress receiving an award at a Powwow with his entourage of more Palefaces than Indians.

"So, Boris Petrovitch," he noted.

"Uncle Boris to his under-aged female employees. Chief Boris to everyone else, in his multicultural family," she pointed out. "Who has connections to many other families elsewhere. On both sides of the legality line, according to all of my research and confidential inquiries."

"And you want me to do what, specifically?" Stevenson inquired, without breaking a sweat or raising an eyebrow.

The deputy's calm demeanor escalated Leona's simmering anger into full rage. She grabbed him by the collar, wishing she could electrify him around the neck instead. From the corner of her eyes, she noted one of the very modern day cameras attached to the wall had paper covering its lens and on the other the lens had been ripped off.

"I want you to give me what I need!" she screamed, not caring if the cameras were on.

"I'll give you what you need if you give me what I need," Stevenson replied, struggling to regain his breath but not too disturbed at losing it.

"And what you need, is what?" she grunted at the

still cool-headed cop while still keeping him at bay. "Money? Dope? A Ukrainian bitch you can call a squaw? A roll in the fucking hay with me!?"

"Air," Stevenson forced out of his mouth with whatever breath he could grab hold of. "Air, please," he asked but did not beg for.

Leona let go of his collar. Seeing her reflection in a mirror, which she hoped was not a two-way, she regained her composure. She wasn't sure why she'd lost it. Maybe it was PTSD left over from the Leon days in the Army, mercenary, or the police force. Or maybe it was righteous indignation from what she'd seen since she returned. In any case, she felt the need to take care of her own biological needs before tending the survival needs of others. She rummaged through her purse looking for the right medication to steady her shaking arms.

"You okay?" Stevenson asked her.

"I'm fine," Leona shot back after she gulped down a blue pill then one red—the white pill falling on the floor then recovered before the mice, rats or any Internal Affairs connected janitor could get hold of it. "I'm just your ordinary, everyday necessary evil," she said by way of explanation for her tone, behavior, and life. She did the anxiety-attack prevention breathing exercises the doctor in Boston said would help lower her blood pressure. Then she moved her finger back and forth in front of her eyes so the left and right brain could reconnect, a suggestion made by her shrink in New Hampshire. "And you, Sheriff Stevenson, are a necessary whatever."

"Hormones?" Stevenson inquired regarding the large pills Leona had in her bag. He looked at her with that calm, collected composure of the psychiatrist who knew everything about brain but nothing about soul.

"What these are is my business," Leona snapped, regarding the collection of medications which were partially prescribed by legal docs and partially formulated by herself as a result of her own knowledge of biology. "I'm risking everything here," she asserted as she zipped her handbag, shutting it with a firm and determined stroke.

"I know," Stevenson said. Before he could elaborate, he heard footsteps coming toward the door. Not three seconds later someone opened it without asking permission to do so.

"Meeting in ten in the conference room, just wanted to let you know in case you forgot," a secretary with legs almost as pretty as Leona's said with a warm smile.

"I didn't forget," Stevenson said. "I just have to finish up with this young lady first."

"Sure, no problem," the secretary replied. She turned around and went on her way, leaving the door open.

From that open door, Leona and Stevenson could see

the whole squad. No doubt the squad cops could see them as well.

“They’re all apples,” Leona said, regarding the Indian on the outside and white on the inside cops.

It wasn’t the first time she’d seen a room full of Law Enforcement Officers more interested in donuts and Christmas bonuses than doing their job. She sensed something very sinister about these Flatfoots, most particularly the ones who had the most pleasant smiles. She always said about any town she visited anywhere in the world that you can’t trust a place until you could see where the garbage is. Though she couldn’t see who was the dirtiest in the Squad room, the aroma of compliance with evil permeated every corner of it.

“I wish I was making the entire thing up,” she shared with Stevenson, sensing that if anyone there could be trusted, it was he. She also knew that without at least one inside man in the cop shop, the plan brewing in her head was doomed for failure. Stevenson seemed too simple to be dangerous or deceptive. But the deputy who wore his heart on the sleeve that still had stains on it from the burger he ate for lunch had to have some skeletons in his closet.

As for what those secrets were, Leona recalled the conversations she just had with her father, along with the research she did on her own through means, she dared not share with her dad for his own good. Tom had said to Leona in passing that Stevenson was a family man who would do anything for his beloved wife but held back as to what he had done or was willing to do. The pieces of the puzzle started to show themselves by the way Stevenson looked at a picture of a young woman whose pale, gaunt face looked prematurely old relative to her eyes.

"I know the difficulty of your position," Leona advanced, going full bore with her best hunch based on the limited intel she had gathered on him. "Your wife died from cancer five years ago, and you couldn't afford the treatment. Today, you still drive an old beater to work. You still buy your food in dollar stores. You watch *Colombo*, *Longmire* and *North of Sixty* on a non-flat-screen used TV that has rabbit ears rather than satellite feed. And your kids are the only two Indians on the Rez who don't walk around in two hundred dollar runners."

"Hmmm… you got most of that right. You did your homework," Stevenson noted as he got up to close the door.

"Om work," Leona replied proudly with a humble Buddhist bow, feeling the sound of that mantra vibrating up and down her spine.

"Huh?" Stevenson replied, not having gotten the joke or the pun, returning to the three and a half-legged chair behind his desk.

"Intellectually and scientifically based humor," Leona explained, once again realizing how alone she was in the world, culturally and otherwise. *Suppose that Einstein and Buddha would have gotten the joke, but as for this realm of reality...* she pondered.

Having been all talked out, she discretely reached into the inside pocket on her coat and pulled out a half-sealed envelope containing a stack of fresh and legal Presidential portraits in it and showed it to Stevenson.

"No one on the Rez or any town within twenty miles of it gets their real money through paychecks," she noted. "But rest assured the money is from me. Hard earned. I was going to use it for my own medical purposes, but there are a whole bunch of girls, young women, and innocent kids of both genders elsewhere who won't grow up to be anything if I don't—"

Stevenson took the envelope. He examined the bills under a lamp with a marker retrieved from his half-broken upper left hand drawer. "It's real all right," he said.

"It shows you're doing your job," Leona replied, in a complimentary manner.

"I miss your brother, Paul. It's a tragedy he died so young."

"And unforgivable that assholes and idiots in this building, and maybe in this room, let it happen, but we are both necessary evils, for each other and the world," she continued, somehow believing it was true. She handed him another envelope. “Instructions,” she said by way of explanation. “From me, your boss in this employment proposition. For you to follow as long as you work for me.”

“Which I will honor as long as we are working for each other and Paul,” Stevenson replied as he put the instruction envelope into his breast pocket. He then stuffed the cash-containing envelope back into Leona’s.

Leona quickly removed it and rammed it back into Stevenson’s hands.

“What I’m asking for is going to be expensive. A winner takes all proposition. With whoever has the balls to do the right thing or is it buy-able to change sides,” Leona pleaded with as much assertiveness as she dared.

A truce emerged between her and Stevenson. After a few reflective moments, the proposition was transformed into an alliance. Just as the necessary miracle between the renegade scientist and the never-left-home cop was about to become full trust, a female officer lower in rank than Stevenson but higher in attitude abruptly opened the door. “Dating again, Deputy Sheriff Stevenson?” Patrol person Karlata McDermott noted with a jealous and watchful eye.

Stevenson tightened his lip, his body tensing up as Karlata entered the room and inspected her boss’s new romantic prospect. “That’s great,” she said, as Leona felt approved of, for the moment anyway. “It looks like you two have a lot in common with each other. And it’s time for you to get involved with someone again,” Karlata said to Stevenson. She then abruptly turned to Leona. “And if I am any judge of character, it seems like it’s time for you to get involved with someone, too.”

Officer Karlata seemed to know a lot about Leona, but then again, as a cop, it was her job to give off that type of an impression. Leona’s job was to give the impression to her new partner, Bill Stevenson, that she knew what she was doing with regard to a plan that would require another layer of trust. It would also require cooperation from someone else she had just met, soul to soul, for the first time in thirty years. That individual sent a text to her phone. It was one of those coincidental accidents that said the Great Spirit was helping or perhaps that life was setting up a vicious practical joke. It was only the second time in Leona’s cyber-phobic father’s life he had ever texted anyone.

“Another birthday package. Red and Black Barn Four PM. Bring what you have, I bring what I kept. Four pm,” Tom texted

CHAPTER 13

The Red and Black Barn was no more than a small cabin deep in the brush. The outside walls were covered by piled up grassy and dirt blending it into the forest. The clandestine multi-purpose Indian-built facility was supposed to have been destroyed along with everyone and everything in it nearly three decades ago.

Upon her arrival, Leona discovered for the last five years Tom had been secretly restoring the barn to its former glory. Her coming home seemed to be the catalyst for him to put that plan into full swing, so its underground doors could be opened for business again.

"These historical artifacts might be useful to you," he said as Leona gawked at the weapons inside the recently opened boxes marked hospital supplies, laundry detergent, and Made in China Authentic Indian headdresses. "Mostly old, some new," Tom continued. He was proudly clad in the faded, blood-stained fringed-leather coat he hadn't worn since he gave up being a Traditional Hunter and Native American activist nearly two decades ago. "These thunder sticks can be used to kill anyone they are pointing at if aimed right. Or… be modified with a Great Grandpa Henry adjustment, they'll—"

"Backfire and kill the sadistic Paleface prick who wants to buy them to murder unarmed Redskin women, children, and old men," Leona interjected, recalling the tall tales out her great grandfather Henry. The ancestor Leona's once-Pacifist Hippie Mom secretly had admired but seldom talked about was a horrible hunter and archer, who knew how to booby trap weapons illegally stolen from them by the Long Knives. Such was the reason why Chief Henry and his renegades defeated the Blue Coats in more than one skirmish.

"Is it your intent to do a Grandpa Henry on the bio-weapons as well as the conventional arms you're giving or selling to Chief Boris?"

"And any other Boris I can fish out of the international muck," Leona replied, regarding the vials of toxins that would do more harm to the people who inflicted them on others than any of their victims. "The antidotes to the bio toxins sold to the bastards who inflict the bio toxins on innocent populations are of course far more deadly than the toxins," she said while proudly viewing them in her very private, overstuffed backpack. "But some of the arms I've purchased with imaginary money will have to work in our hands. For us." She picked up one of the thunder sticks in Tom's collection then a twenty-first century shooting iron Carlos had sent the most recent care package. "We'll need some functioning weapons to liberate sex slaves who I fear may be beyond being liberated if we wait too long. And as I do have to ask, how many of 'us' can you activate?"

"I'm not as influential in that area as I used to be," Tom replied with downturned eyes, which conveyed his being ashamed, angry, and betrayed. "I can't give you an Army of Warrior Indians willing to stand up for what is ours. That you'll have to get on your own. Only be sure that the fire you breathe out of your mouth doesn't come back to burn your ass or roast to a crisp those who you care about most."

Leona had so many questions to ask Tom. She yearned to know what he really did when he was an activist back in the seventies and eighties. She needed to know why he went dormant. One of the answers was in front of her face, directly behind the once-broad shoulders of the man who she thought would not crouch them for anyone. It was the picture of Tom, Emily, and their two happy, carefree five and six-year-old kids surrounded by cats, dogs, and horses in a canvas bordered by trees and sunshine. That very non-political snapshot was the image Leona held onto so tightly in her heart to get her through the hardest of times elsewhere. Now it seemed like a distant dream, unobtainable by anyone in her family. But there were girls and women enslaved by Boris et al who still could go back to the golden times they enjoyed before their abduction. The possibility of that has-to-be-made-real-dream prompted Leona to ask Tom about the weapons he dug up from his days as a radical activist.

Tom told Leona everything about the weapons dating from 1898 Winchesters to Vietnam War surplus semi-automatic rifles, along with a few more modern pieces that found their way to him as collector's items at gun and knife shows. He put a small yellow mark on the ones that were intended to backfire on their buyers. Green dots went on the ones that would be dysfunctional after several trials at the firing range. White dots signified those Leona could use if she could find an army of Leon's willing to carry on the fight that Tom could only support from behind.

"A group of three hundred Spartans armed with the right position held back an Army of ten thousand Persians. With these, and an army of two, you could hold back Chief Boris's army of thugs and goons," Tom said to his Comrade Daughter and former son.

"I was thinking an Army of three, me, Stevenson, and you," Leona replied, pushing Tom for an answer.

Tom directed her to a more recent photo of her mother, Emily. His now frumpy, born-again-Christian and scared of anything outside of the bell shaped curve wife had that the "I see nothing and want to stay out of everything" look in her face.

"I understand you have to do what you have to do and have to honor pledges to protect people you are responsible for. And who, at one time, you even loved," Leona said to her father.

Leona's remark seemed to hit Tom straight between the eyes. He replied with an all-knowing smile then a look in his face that said it was time for another tall tale about his ancestors and Leona's. "Sitting Bull was too old to fight at Little Big Horn, but he was a master at getting intel, from both the world everyone could see and the realms most people couldn't see," he related. "It was his job to keep getting intel while Crazy Horse and the others rode into the Little Big Horn valley and finally gave Custer what he deserved. With rifles that were not that much different than these here, Leona,"

"Yes, I know, but there's one problem with that story."

"That real world intel is different than a Vision?" Tom asked.

"That the Blue Coats were a lot harder on us after we whooped Custer than beforehand. And that all of your blood is Indian and only half of mine is," Leona replied. "And that Mom's great grandfather, as I found out when I looked into it just recently, was a Paleface Blue Coat Cavalry Officer who enjoyed killing a lot of Indians after Little Big Horn before he went back East and became respectable. I'm not sure if Mom knows about that. Should I tell her?"

"Ignorance is bliss," Tom replied after an even deeper reflected pause. "And a lot safer," he said of the wife he apparently pitied, feared, had been abandoned by, but still no doubt, deeply loved.

CHAPTER 14

The sign over the casino door read “Closed for Religious Holiday” in English and Cree. Inside everything was open for business, and business was booming. Finally, Leona was given access to the large supply room in the building she remembered as always being empty. It was hardly empty now. With her escort and new business partner, Chief Boris, she walked up and down the rows of wares for sale. They were spread out on tables and displayed in the same manner as the top quality pharmaceutical companies and research supply corporations did at every neuroscience meeting she had attended.

Everything supplied by Boris or Leona was clean, spotless, and presented with the most professional appearance possible. Prominently featured were firearms and bio-toxins for top dollar. The displayers and refreshment servers could be purchased or loaned out for a dollar a poke. Yolanda 2 and Amanda 4 were among the sales staff. Their beautifully made-up faces revealed their broken spirits to anyone who cared to really look into them. They, as well as the other nieces on display to the perspective uncles from all corners of the globe, had one thing in common aside from un-removable fashion collars around their neck—a despondent what the fuck, I don’t care anymore attitude toward everything. If

Leona's plan was to work, they had to be made to care again about something.

She pondered the matter from an equine perspective, thinking about the case of Nemo, a horse broken into subservience then blind obedience by Hank Ralston, a super macho bubba-bellied rancher who fancied himself to be Clint Eastwood. Anyone human could get on Nemo's back and make him do anything. When it came to feeding time, any horse that wanted Nemo's ration of grain always got it. It was only after Granny had worked with him from the inside that Nemo gained back some of his self-respect by tossing Hank Ralston out of the saddle when he returned to take him for a spin to impress his new Indian Princess girlfriend. From that day onward, Nemo belonged to Granny and himself.

For every Nemo the horse, there was a Rodney the rodent. Rodney was a rat that Leona's thesis adviser had trained as a model for human depression, aka learned helplessness. The procedure to produce it was easy. A normal rodent put into a tank of water with a submerged platform will swim to it and save itself, time and time again without delay. Then you put him in a mildly electrified maze where he was offered the chance to get a chunk of cheese if he could figure his way out. Whenever the rat found to escape to reach the cheese, the door would be closed on the latter. After it was done to Rodney and his rodent pals long enough, they were put into the water tank inches away from the submerged platform. The last time, they chose to sink instead of save themselves. Leona hoped there were more Rodney's than Nemo's amongst the many slaves Boris had spread throughout the arms and flesh-selling fare in the warehouse behind the Casino.

Looking around, she felt empowered somehow, as if the Great Spirit was with her. Perhaps it was merely the ghost of Granny who was with her as she saw the first participant in that plan enter the door with his entourage. The test for that hypothesis swaggered into the door.

General Timolto was built and walked like an Afro-American inner city gangster. Stripped down to his birthday suit above the neck, but he was a fat pig whose face looked like a bulldog with a sloped forehead typical of a born-to-be-dumb beer-drinking slob. Yet, dressed in his African country's Military Uniform, he looked powerful, smart, and even handsome. He eyed with equal interest the firearms from Boris's collection, Leona's secret suppliers abroad and Tom's underground stash. Timolto had a special affinity for Amanda 4 and Yolanda 2, primo white meat that would please his very African palate.

"Impressive merchandise, Boris," the fat, dark-skinned African General commented to his thin white Russian host regarding the human specimens for sale. "Who are not smiling," he noted.

“Apologies, General,” Colonel Petrovitch said with a courtly bow. He discretely motioned for his thugs to do the appropriate adjustments. The two thugs behind Boris pressed the remote-control devices hidden in their pockets, causing a jolt to awaken Yolanda 2 and Amanda 4 out of their glazed, despondent modes. Boris gave them an angry stare, motioning with his lips for them to smile. They didn’t do so.

Apparently angry, Boris gave Yolanda 2 and Amanda 4 that “you know what I do to girls who embarrass me in front of my clients” stare. The high-priced pleasure girls looked back at Boris with that “we have nothing else to lose” look in their faces Leona recalled experiencing first hand on more occasions than she could count, both as Leon and Leona. Boris’s goons reached for their electro-zappers in their pocket. Before they could turn them to full bore, Leona intervened.

“Hold off!” she said to the electro enforces. “I’ll remind these Nemo bitches they’d be happier as obedient Rodney’s,” she pledged to Boris. Without bothering to explain the meaning of the descriptors, Leona pulled her chin up and strode up to the two girls. She slapped both of them then looked down on them with a power-dominatrix stare. Before they could shoot back defiance with their eyes or bow their heads in surrender, Leona loosened the top buttons on their blouses and adjusted their cleavage. Into the latter she inserted a key. "Smile for those assholes now, fuck them up the ass in ten minutes on your way back to your own lives," she whispered to each of them, amidst a few more dominatrix slaps that excited Timolto and pleased Boris. Then she snuck a mini Carlos-special semi-automatic pistol into the private place that had been violated so many times between their legs. "Use this on whoever you have to."

Yolanda 2 smiled at her master, Boris, and his buddy, Timolto. "Thank you for the steak," she whispered to Leona, apparently recognizing Leona as the guest doctor who came into the dormitory the day when they were finally fed a full meal for the first time in weeks. She nudged her fellow slave sister Amanda 4 to smile for Chief Boris and the black General, which she did. Boris seemed satisfied. Timolto seemed pleased. Leona joined them.

"As you can see, General, everything you need for your Revival Revolution is here to arm your men and to keep them entertained between victories," the Russian boss said to his potential African client and perhaps one day temporary ally. "Without any medical or psychological complications."

"Yes, I see they are healthy specimens, well fed and in good non-disease carrying conditions," Timolto conceded. "They are worth at least double what you are asking for."

"I told you that you could get more money for these gals if you feed them well and give them medications from my special stash," Leona whispered to Boris. "You owe me one."

"But," Timolto interjected, turning around quickly to face Boris before he could give a reply to Leona. "You said there would be weapons for sale here that did not require bullets."

"Which are right this way," Leona smiled, bowing to the African War Lord even deeper than Boris did. Such was of course necessary as women were an inferior species relative to men in Timolto's world, even if those women were smarter than the men who owned them.

With a seductive wiggle of her ass, Leona led the General and his entourage across the room. Her tour brought them around and through the less affluent and less dangerous buyers attending the fair who were more concerned with metallic killing devices than the biological ones that were most deadly. The final destination was a table where she had displayed her special mass population inactivating compounds along with antidotes. Each was coded with a number and color. Boris stayed in the background while Leona displayed the wares at the only table hosted by no nieces and manned by none of Boris's uncles.

"It is my pleasure, and honor, General, to bring to you with my new associate Colonel Petrovitch, the newest biological tools to treat the political and social diseases you are endeavoring to eradicate," Doctor Leona said.

"Toxins and microbes that can inactivate specific targets at specific intervals," Boris added.

"Indeed," Leona continued. She felt herself a player in a guy/gal used car commercial in which Boris was the guy who made the claims and she was the gal who assured the viewer with a wide grin and nod that everything her man said was gospel. All of that would, of course, bedazzle the buyer until he signed the check then broke down in the parking lot after driving out the deal of the year. "And we feature for each of our state of the art bio toxins, antidotes to protect those who are entrusted to inactivate your enemy's targets. As well as, most importantly, to protect you and you're most entrusted family members from any accidental or intentional exposure."

Leona offered Timolto a sniff of the antidotes after pretending to take a whiff in herself. While Timolto inhaled the protective agents into his very large nostrils, she noticed other buyers at the indoor shooting range getting ready to sample the wares they wanted to buy. They would be allowed to test those weapons on dummy targets. All of them bore the likenesses of civilian women, children, and old men, according to Boris's instruction and Leona's timetable.

"Yes," Timolto said, displaying his satisfaction with a carefree grin, featuring a mouth full of white teeth and regarding the aroma of the antidotes. "Have a sniff, Boris. This is quite an enjoyable aroma! Good medicine that tastes good too."

The normally very austere General laughed with unbridled passion and bliss, all according to Leona's timetable. On Leona's signal, Yolanda 2 attempted to use the key Leona had given her. She discreetly unlocked her collar then Amanda 4's. Both of them circulated around the other nieces, unlocking their shock collars not being detected. All was still according to Leona's timetable.

"You have to try this antidote!" Timolto said to Boris with the happy glow of a stoner. He gave his Russian host sample of his favorite powdered antidote to sample. "Every painful part of my body and mind is feeling so good now!"

Leona nodded for Boris to accept the General's offer. He hesitated. "I have to hold on to my pain," Boris told the General by way of explanation.

"But I insist," the General said. "Your female associate was gracious enough to join me in a sniff. And since you are lacking in manners, I have no choice but to—"

Timolto snapped his fingers, commanding every gun carried by an African to be aimed at Boris's goons then at Boris himself. Most of Boris's goons replied by aiming their weapons at Timolto and his men. Everyone else at the fare, excluding the slaves, backed up against the walls. They took shelter or bet on who would still be standing after the next macho insult.

"Oh yeah," Leona said, taking on the persona of an ecstatic stoner and soon-to-be happy drunk. "My associate, Boris, knows that sharing a good drink with an old friend such as you is part of doing business."

"Like sharing a good-looking woman after the business is over?" Timolto said with a bellowing laugh. He pulled Leona close in to him with his humongous left arm. Then he brought Boris into the group hug with his large apelike left. "The three of us party after this is over, yes?" he bellowed out while holding both Boris and Leona hostage in his happy place.

"Yes, we will both enjoy Leona's company, as she will enjoy ours," Boris said to the African General. He gazed at Leona like she should be honored to be the featured feast at the gentlemen's table.

Timolto said something to the fellow Africans amongst the mixed congregation that made them lower their weapons then their guard. Boris ordered his men to lower their arms as well.

"This is a party, enjoy the merchandise," Boris reminded his men in Russian and English, after which each of the armed uncles grabbed hold of a niece.

Timolto repeated what was no doubt meant the same thing in his language, his men doing the same.

The menfolk talked amongst themselves as to who would get what woman flesh. Boris wasn't happy when he saw Leona was worried. He was enraged when he saw the two guards assigned the duty of looking after the West and South exit doors distracted by nieces coming on to their new uncles in a game the nieces seemed to be controlling.

There were some things that didn't anger nor concern Boris as the rest of Leona's secret plan proceeded. He didn't even break a sweat when he heard police sirens everywhere around the building that sent the buyers into fear for their lives, accusations for them being there directed at their host. He was un-rattled at the three excessively armed bikers thinly disguised as an army of cops who came storming into the room after Amanda 4 and one of the newer nieces opened the door for them. He didn't bat an eye at the backfiring weapons at the shooting range blowing the heads off the foreign buyers and his own goons who were shooting them. Boris also took in stride when General Timolto abruptly coughed up blood. The African whipped out his own pistol then aimed it at a still cool-headed Boris. Timolto was unable to pull the trigger due to a full-blown epileptic seizure that landed him on the floor, thanks to the delayed effect of the aromatic antidote Leona had provided a sample sniff.

Leona didn't stick around Boris long enough for him to ask her what was going on and what had gone wrong in the intricate plan she had devised herself. The biggest thing that went wrong, of course, was that she had inadvertently saved Boris's life by poisoning a client who was about to kill him. Ducking for cover to see what else was happening according to plan or accident, she looked around for Stevenson. Thankfully he was by the North exit, along with Amanda 4 and Yolanda 2. They were ushering twenty liberated nieces toward the door before more dummy sirens were set off outside. Meanwhile the Africans and Russians kept trying to kill each other. Each group thought they were set up by the other. The smaller league gangs and cartels in between tried to save their own asses by aligning with whoever was closest to them amidst the gunfire.

It was a perfect set up and liberation, until Yolanda 2 had a change of heart after seeing the sun for the first time since her abduction. She yearned for the security of confinement again, grabbing Stevenson's gun upon returning to the escape door and pointing it at him.

"I came back for you, Chief Boris," she yelled out to her slave master across the room in her best English. "And give you present of this officer," she said of Stevenson. "And that woman you think you know is not who you think she is," she continued, aiming the gun at

Leona, and firing.

Before the second shot could go off, Stevenson grabbed hold of the pistol Yolanda 2's hand. Through the open door, a wounded and unable to walk Leona watched Amanda 4 pull Yolanda 2 back outside, punching her in the stomach. Amanda 4 worked with the other girls to get Yolanda 2 into the escape vehicle before she could reveal anything more about Leona.

A stray bullet from the mob war hit Leona's right arm, making her lose all abilities to hold onto anything. Wounded in the arm and the leg, she was unable to effectively move, but that didn't matter. Boris wasn't moving either. He was hit by one of the African's bullets in his leg. Resolved yet again to his fate, he drank the vodka from his pocket flask, singing one of his "it's a good day to die" songs in Russian.

Death after a lifetime of wearing a dog collar around your neck in jail is how wanted it, but I'll take what I can get, Leona said to herself, satisfied her life had been worth all of the agonies, all of the hardships. She motioned for Stevenson to move the girls out quickly, and that she would join them soon. It would be in the afterlife, which was okay with Leona.

As if on schedule, a third shot came from somewhere unidentifiable that grazed Leona's head; she fell to the floor, seeing black in front of her face then a bright light. She heard the escalating gunfire dissolve into deafening silence, the gentle sound of a summer's day, and the even gentler sound of Granny's voice. The Old Sage whose spirit was always young called out to her in Cree words she did not understand but felt to be assuring.

The transition acquired a deeper dimension as Leona entered the Spirit World, the huya aniya according to the Yaqui Indians in Northwest Mexico. According to theory, and some personal experience, it was a realm that affected the real world and vice versa.

Leona felt herself as teenaged Leon, riding a horse next to his brother. Both of them had recently sprouted pubic hair on their genitals and respectable non-peach fuzz mustaches on their lips. Their hair was long. Their shirtless bodies were wrapped in leather-fringed leggings which complimented their moccasins. They were herding cows across the ranch they were hired to look after for the owner. The cows turned into buffalo. Just when young Leon and Paul felt the herd of buffalo moving as one unit, directed by their horses, something in the brush spooked the steeds. The herd of bison scattered. The horses reared up. For the moment, the riders stayed on top of them

"What's happening, man?" Leon asked Paul.

"I don't know," Paul replied. "These horses see something we don't?"

"A fucking bear, maybe," Leon speculated.

"A goddamn ghost," Paul said as his proud-cut

gelding bolted away at a full gallop.

"I can't hold on!" Leon screamed as his horse attempted to do the same. "She's trying to rear up on me."

"Then let go," Leon heard from Granny in Cree then English from behind a clump of trees. She strolled up next to Leon as he struggled to stay atop his frightened mare. "Or give her a swift kick in the ass and make her go where you want her to," Granny calmly suggested as she adjusted the strap on her herb collecting bag, tasting the berries about to be collected for medicinal extractions.

Leon squeezed his knees together, worked the reins, and somehow got the mare to move ahead in a circle that was, for the most part, in a path of his design. Three revolutions around the rosy later, the mare seemed to calm down. Just when Leon moved his hand to the mare's neck to give it a "thank you for not killing me" pat, a gust of wind blew threw a clump of trees, following a beam of blinding light which terrified horse and rider.

"Astum, Leon," Granny said from the other side of the whirling, light-infused trees. "Come forward into it," she commanded.

"I can't!" Leon answered.

"You can," Granny assured him, becoming a beacon of light herself. "But it's your choice, nobody else's," she assured him. She whisked her hand in front of the horse then said some words Leon didn't understand. Apparently the frightened mare understood what she said and obeyed her.

The horse laid its front feet firmly on the ground, eased its back muscles, and calmly waited for Leon to command it to move forward or backward.

Just then, Leon heard something from the bush. He recognized it as the finale to Wagner's *Gotterdammerung*, otherwise known as *The Twilight of the Gods*.

Leon recalled the Legend of Brunhilde, who at the end of the four-hour opera decided that she and the rest of humanity had been given enough shit from the gods. It was time for her to ride her horse, Grain, into the fires of Valhalla and give them the third finger salute. It was a gesture to the fates that would cost Brunhilde own life but give life back to humanity.

"I'm ready," Leon asserted as he nudged his horse onward to destroy darkness and become light.

"Not yet," Granny said, holding her hands out in front.

"Grain" reared up and tossed Leon onto the ground. He rolled down a hill leading to a cliff, his fall stopped by a body lying in the grass. Leon was shocked when he saw what and who it was.

"Yes, she is you, and you are her, and you are each

other," Granny smiled as she strolled over to him. "Leon, meet Leona. Leona, meet Leon," she said to the body of the male and female expressions of the soul who was named Leon at birth because he bore a penis in his present incarnation.

The very naked and beautiful Leona invited Leon to embrace him with a warm, welcoming smile.

"Who is that? What is that?" Leon said, terrified.

"An opportunity," Granny explained. "For you to be the most effective person you can be."

"But I'm not a pervert," Leon asserted.

"No," Granny assured him. "You're something even more dangerous. You are special. Gifted."

"A necessary evil," Leon said. "Who will take on the revolution for human rights for Indian people my father abandoned or can't fight anymore?"

"Who will do more good with or as Leona, than as you, Leon," Granny said. "But if you don't believe me, ask your horse."

On cue, the horse walked over to Leon, nudged him then turned to its side, positioning itself so Leon could easily mount him, which he didn't.

"Or ask the light in the bush," Granny suggested as the fire in the bush turned from being a hellish wall to a Heavenly beacon. "Or ask him," Granny continued, regarding the expression of the Great Spirit up in the sky.

A realization hit Leon. "The Great Spirit isn't a him or a her. It's—"

"—Beyond and within both of us," Leona interjected. She emerged from the ground and stood proudly in front of Leon. She handed him the hanging reins, which were still attached to the bridle still attached to the horse.

"Yes, indeed," Leon smiled. He gave Leona a leg up on the horse. Then got up on the saddle behind her. Leon allowed his body to merge into Leona's. Together they nudged Grain onward. Horse and the merged riders galloped into the light, merging into infinity. The merged soul felt light and heavy, both at the same time. Then it asked Granny, in Leona's voice, one question.

"Where am I?"

CHAPTER 15

Leona slowly opened her eyes and realized she was in the hospital. Wagner played on a small transistor radio on the table next to her hospital bed. The visitor sitting next to her adjusted the dial in an attempt to make the NPR station from Bismarck come across stronger than the Top Forty broadcasts from local outlets on both sides of the band.

"What happened?" Leona slurred as a sudden winter-like breeze filtered through the partially opened window, blowing her hospital gown up toward her chest. She covered herself up as quickly as she could. The male visitor sitting at her bedside continued to read his newspaper.

"Welcome back," Stevenson said with a sincere welcoming tone. "We missed you."

"Maybe some of you did," Leona replied, wanting to get a closer look at the headlines on the newspaper and the picture under it. "What happened when I was… away?"

Stevenson moved the paper out of her field of vision but not the grasp of her uninjured left hand and very well repaired right arm. Indeed, the blurry image she saw of it was very real, in crystal-clear black and white. "Chief Boris Elected Honorary Elder Inter-tribal Leader," it read. The photo featured Boris' smiling mug under a full headdress war bonnet while accepting the esteemed award which had not been given to a white man since Kevin Costner did *Dances with Wolves*.

Leona turned her angry eyes toward Stevenson's gentle ones. "I thought you were supposed to—"

"Arrest me?" Boris mused, walking into the room with a bandage around his injured leg. There was only slight trace of a limp in his stride, indicating to Leona that either it really was just a flesh wound or that the limb was repaired better than new by the best doc's human trafficking profits could buy off. "It was Deputy Sheriff Stevenson's job to arrest me," Chief Boris smirked as Stevenson got out of his chair, said throne taken by the Russian Kingpin. "Just as it was my job to stand up for my legal rights. And it was the job of my Indian lawyers to do their job to defend me. You know, you people make better lawyers than buffalo hunters."

Boris whipped out a bouquet of flowers from behind his coat. He presented them to Leona with a kind, inviting smile. She took them, cautiously. Not two seconds later, with a snap of his fingers, Boris dismissed Stevenson. Stevenson left the room with a humbly bowed head. Boris took over his post next to Leona's bed. He turned the radio to one of the country music stations, on which there was a song she hated because of its simplistic church-going lyrics. They were made demonic by Boris singing them in Russian.

"What happened in the casino at the trade show?" she asked.

"To the African General?" Boris asked. "You eliminated a problem for me. I can always get more generals who want to be gods."

"And the girls? The real money making merchandise?" Leona inquired, doing her best to come off as a sex slave trafficker.

"I don't know how they got out, but you don't either, do you?" he asked, turning off the radio.

"No, I don't," Leona replied, doing her best to put on a poker face.

"In any case, if you were trying to burrow them from me or they found their own way out on their own, I—no we—will be remarketing them soon, after they have been appropriately re-educated," Boris assured her. He opened Stevenson's newspaper to the funnies section. "And besides, who is going to believe the stories my girls say about me or you? No one of any importance will believe them anyway. No unimportant people a few of them ran into believed them, either."

"Yeah, that's good to know," she replied, pretending to not care about the merchandize but aching for them on the inside more than she ever had.

"You are still of very importance to me, my dear, Leona," Boris said in the "family" way. He turned around, inspecting her body through the hospital gown with his X-ray vision.

"Even though I can't, ya know…?" she replied.

"Have children?"

"I have… problems in that area. Had to have some of my reproductive machinery removed," Leona said, doing her best to invent a lie on the fly that wouldn't nose dive into a crash. "Accidental exposure to a cancer-causing virus I developed that was supposed to be sold to a two-bit dictator who wanted to sterilize woman of inferior races in and around his country," she said, anticipating what was not found in any X-ray taken of her after admission to the hospital. "Asking my private physician to take out my uterus saved my life and made it easier to have a thinner girlish figure," Leona mused, recalling that though her penis was small, it was still very noticeable. "So any hope of you and me making little Leona's and Boris's to populate the world in our image is a bygone daydream."

"This is… good," Boris concluded. "Less complications in the nursery and more fun in the bedroom."

"And about my female parts… they're still there," she added, hoping Boris really didn't have any idea of what was still between her legs.

"From where I see it, you are more woman than any girl I ever bought or any Madame who sold them to me." He smiled, gazing at her breasts.

Boris bent over and kissed her on the lips. He kept his eyes closed—Leona kept hers open. Boris snapped his fingers again then waved Stevenson back into the room.

"Deputy Stevenson, you take good care of her or I will have your job," he instructed the lawman who Leona's father had said was too caring to be corruptible. "And Leona," Boris continued, putting his big bear-like paws proudly on the sheepish deputy's slumped shoulders. "This is a good man."

"Yes, a good man," she repeated, as Boris always liked it when people repeated the opinions he voiced as universal law.

"A man who knows his place!" Boris boasted regarding his new protégée, Stevenson, whose eyes continued to look down to the floor. "He embraces his responsibilities and accepts his limitations."

"Yes, he does," Leona concluded and conceded.

"But, Sheriff Stevenson, perhaps Police Commissioner Stevenson," Boris said, commanding his new student to look him in the eye, man to man. "Remember that this woman is mine to love and yours to protect? Yes?"

"Da," Stevenson nodded.

Boris seemed pleased. He ended the visit with a hearty "there ya go, partner" slap on Stevenson's back, which the deputy somehow managed to keep upright.

Chief Boris then took his coat, the newspaper, and walked out of the room.

Stevenson looked at Leona, after hearing the elevator and seeing Boris had entered it and the door closed on him. “Explanations, Leona. Which you are entitled to.”

Stevenson closed the door then strolled around the room somehow back in control of himself. He searched for any hidden microphones Boris may have left behind. For the moment, he didn’t find any. Still, he talked in a hushed voice to the background of the most obnoxious happy song he could find on the radio.

“As for what is still between your legs, only one dude here and two nurses know about it. The doc who took care of you has a file at the cop shop that says he’s a cross dresser among other things. He wants to have a consult with you after about fitting high fashion around fat bodies and how to deal with his wife who knows nothing about the other life. The two nurses I had to pay off with some, actually a lot, of the spending money you gave me. One of them will pray for your soul at church this Sunday. And as for Boris—”

“You want more money to not tell him what and who I really am, Commissioner Stevenson?” Leona interjected.

“No,” Stevenson replied, finally convinced they were alone, not being watched, or listened to. He turned off the radio, as irritated with the Dancing Blackfoot

Princess Redneck top forty hit as Leona was.

"So, tell me for Christ and Buddha's sake what went wrong in there with the plan that you were supposed to put in place, and my father Tom did his best to…"

The mention of Tom's name turned Stevenson's probing eyes into sorrowful ones.

"What happened to my father?" she demanded.

"Gone," Stevenson replied, staring intensely out the window. "To where, I don't know. Along with your mother," he related and confessed.

"And the last place anyone saw either of them was where?" Leona pressed.

"Home," Stevenson replied. He turned to Leona. Sincerity oozed out of his eyes in a way she had never seen in him, or for that matter, in any other man she had encountered since she decided to become a woman. "Home. A place you and I can never go back to unless we both get solidly cooperative, really smart, and very, very lucky."

CHAPTER 16

Tom's and Emily's house had fewer conveniences than most of the others on the Rez that had been modernized after the Arrowhead Casino came into town, but it was a far sight more twenty-first century than it was when Leona left. More by necessity than choice. Leona's mother hadn't aged as well in appearance as her father Tom had, perhaps because she was white or maybe because she was a woman. Tom had done what he could to see that the dwelling they lived in was as beautiful as she once had been back in the Flower Power hippie days. Emily's arthritis and other afflictions in the last decade limited her wilderness activity to walks in the woods with a cane rather than gallops across the mountains on horseback. Such prompted Tom to be sure the house was easy to get around in and climate controlled no matter what the weather was doing outside. But now it looked like a tornado had hit it, whirling up its most fierce winds from the inside. Nothing that was on the walls remained there. Every drawer was opened, not a single piece of glass un-shattered.

"This is what we found after the call came in," Stevenson said to Leona when he took her into what had been a living room now littered with valuables that were now nothing but debris.

"The call from who?" she inquired.

"Tina Bear," Stevenson said. "Who was entertaining someone other than her husband at the time, which required that the call be anonymous."

"To protect herself or her husband?" Leona pressed.

"Both," Stevenson replied.

It was the correct answer with regard to Tina's libido and the misplaced love she still had for a husband who thought she was the only one. He would certainly kill himself if he found out he wasn't.

Convinced he gave the right answer to Leona, Stevenson went on. "According to what Tina saw, there were some guys in black ski masks who came in, some through the front door, some through the back. Another two through entered through the side the windows. Then there was some arguing. Some screaming. And some shooting. Then two bodies wrapped in blankets were put into back seat of Tom's truck by three guys wearing large visor hats and sunglasses. The truck pulled away in a quiet cloud of exhaust. Outside of that, Tina didn't see very much. She wanted to say more, but after she got a call from her daughter, she didn't."

"Well, what do you say?" she asked.

"That maybe we're the only two people left here who can trust each other." he proposed. "And that in the official report the getaway car crashed over the side of the only real cliff on Thunder Mountain where they were chased by cops for reckless driving is both inaccurate and fabricated."

"Is that a question or an answer?"

"Both. But can I ask you one question first, Leona?"

"Why the fuck not?"

Stevenson pondered the matter for a tense moment then turned to Leona. "How well did you really know your brother?" he asked, inviting her to open up her heart to him regarding the matter.

Leona looked down at the debris on the floor. Her stare was held hostage by the photos of her and Paul, arm in arm, as best buds. The torn but not destroyed snapshots captured the magic, and reality, from the time they were knee high to Tom's stuffed bear to the time when they went out hunting for bear on their own two feet. Leona found herself recalling that upon her return to the Rez Granny also asked her how well Leona knew Paul or was prepared to know him.

"So, you and Paul. How well did you really know him?" Stevenson asked, demanding an answer this time. Though his arms were folded, his heart was open.

"Not as well as you and Granny think I should, and maybe in ways I never wanted to."

Stevenson led her through what was left of the door to the basement then down a staircase into what had been Tom's private bear cave. The stairs were still intact but nothing downstairs was. The computer and all of the equipment and drives associated with it were gone, everything around it in disarray. Every bit of electronic cyber or surveillance equipment was gone or pulverized. Amongst the pile of debris were half-century old vinyl records, most of which were surprisingly intact.

"I heard Tom was a fan of Jefferson Airplane before they became Jefferson Starship," Stevenson said as he pulled out the faded cover of the *Lather* album.

"And before they became Yuppie sell outs," Leona recalled. "My father said if he could ever find Gracey Slick, he'd do an intervention with her to remind her how innovative she was in her youth, and that it isn't too late to go forward to that golden past and—"

Before she could recall the rest of the golden memory, Stevenson pulled a photograph out of the Airplane album and handed it to her. "The CSI team didn't find this, I hope. Thank our lucky stars and Starships I did."

"I don't believe it!" Leona gasped as her jaw dropped to the floor.

"It's just a picture, but it's very suggestive."

"My brother Paul on a fishing trip with Boris? Both of them smiling like they're best buds!" Leona exclaimed, regarding the photo of the two men with a fish in the middle of them that was taller than them both. "This proves nothing!"

"But this does," Stevenson replied. He turned over

the picture, pointing to the date it was taken.

"Two years before Boris was seen here with anyone else?"

"I found other photos with both of them together, doing things a lot more illegal and cooperative than fishing without a license during the off season," Stevenson said. "I found some of them in some old boxes in the garage, and a few others in the evidence room that I took before they—"

"I want to see them!" blasted back through a lump in her throat, trying her best to direct her anger and overcome her grief. "No, I need to see them," she continued, coming back to her senses.

"I know you do, but not here," Stevenson said with an assuring voice. He pointed her attention to a police car cruising the street outside on "routine" rounds.

Leona ushered Stevenson and herself out the only still-functional secret exit doors in the basement she, Paul, and her father had built. It led to a small underground cavern, which opened up thankfully to still-thick brush beyond Tom's property. They then proceeded as quietly as possible under a bright moonlit sky to Stevenson's private beater truck, which he had parked three blocks away amidst a clump of trees. It afforded them a clear view of the driveway of the house, in which one cruiser was parked, joined by two other police cars and a black sedan with tainted glass.

"We're going after them, now!" she grunted. "Even if no one else will," she continued, noting the shades on every window with a view of the house were being drawn closed the lights behind them turned off.

"And wind up like Grandpa Uncle Henry did?" Stevenson said.

Leona recalled the story about how her legendary Warrior Ancestor met his end. Yes, it was a matter of honor to attack two hundred Blue Coats with seven fellow warriors upon seeing their commander rape his wife, but it was also a trap.

"If all of Uncle Grandpa Henry's war party decided to do a suicide mission, Tom and you would have not been born," he continued, opening the passenger door for Leona as a genuinely kind and terrified gentleman. "And if Henry could speak from the grave he'd say—"

"Attack when your brain says it's time, not when your heart or temper says," Leona interjected. With that, she got into the truck, allowing Stevenson to close the door for her.

CHAPTER 17

Leona couldn't get the pictures of Paul and Boris out of her head. Logic told her she should concern herself with why those pictures were still in existence. Reason told her it was essential to find out why they were found in Tom's and Emily's house ten years after Paul had left home. If indeed Paul had converted over to the dark side, why did he do so? And did he do it willingly? Leona also allowed herself to consider as fact her most hopeful speculation—that Paul was working undercover for the good guys to get the goods on what Boris was up to so he could nap the Russian Godfather with as many other Godfathers as possible.

There was some evidence for that wildest and most welcomed speculation. Though Paul was known as the most honest Injun in town who never got get away with telling a lie on the Rez; he fancied himself to be a First Nations James Bond. He was an avid fan of any espionage flick on the tube. He even tried his hand writing a series of novels about *Injun Joe* an Uncle Tom sellout to his tribe back in the nineteenth century who headed east to Washington in 1860. Injun Joe worked behind the scenes by planting false intel so the North and South would go to war with each other sooner rather than later. Such would keep as many Palefaces East of the Mississippi or buried in early graves as possible, sabotage any attempt of the North and South to not go to war with each other. The plan backfired after 1865 when the worse elements of the once proud Armies came west eager to steal from the Indians what their fellow Palefaces had stolen from them. Injun Joe redeemed himself when he hired himself as an Indian scout who secretly brought Custer intel about how he could whoop the Sioux at Little Big Horn in one, swift blow.

No one took Paul's literary ventures seriously, perhaps because he was a worse writer than liar. Or perhaps because he thought too big and bold in a world where people who thought small and obediently were the ones who got ahead. All of that would be dealt with later.

Logic now took a back seat to physical survival. Leona could not go back to her hotel room. It was one of those hunches she had, as well as a warning Stevenson gave her, particularly after he showed her the picture of her rental car. It had been impounded by his fellow officers and scrutinized even more than her abducted parents' pad. Emotional survival was also something that had to be maintained now Leona felt like an orphan. Though Leona was easily sustained by being alone; it terrified her.

Stevenson's mobile bachelor cave was a logical place to hold up to figure out the next step, emotionally and otherwise. Leona sat on the only spot not taken up by clutter in the poorly-insulated trailer. Through a mouth fear had made salty and anger had made dry, she sipped coffee that tasted more like the no-name cardboard box it came from than real java.

"You don't have anything stronger? Or deadly? You have to!" she grunted, seeking to numb all of the pain inside of her. That pain very much included knowing she had been a "Boris" while being Leon back in the good old mercenary days.

True, there were days where Leon and Boris liberated ten oppressed victims of one sort of another from bad guys. At the same time they were working for higher-ups, who were oppressing hundreds and thousands behind the scenes. Dark nights that followed those days were made celebratory with the best dope and booze that was steal-able or unofficially lost before they went into the evidence room or the incinerator.

As for the darkened day Leona was having now, Stevenson didn't make it any brighter with his slowpoke, procedural way of doing everything. The more agitated she got inside, the calmer he seemed to be, and perhaps the less caring. The more her cold hands trembled, the more he went about the business of cleaning up normal bachelor clutter like it was just another day at the beach.

"I said, Deputy Dawg Stevenson," she grunted, trying to stay awake and alert. Even a blind man could see she was in legitimate need of a rocket fuel good girls and boys never put into their engines. “Don’t you have anything stronger than this fucking, lame, plain-Jane black coffee?”

Stevenson abruptly stopped filing loose papers into appropriate drawers and garbage cans according to his personally-designed non-linear filing system. Finally, she’d got his attention.

“Something stronger, let’s see,” he replied, with his back still turned to her. After two deep breaths, he turned to her. “Stronger medicine for aching souls, sure,” he said with a tone she thought he was never capable of sarcasm. He rummaged through every cabinet within reach for what Leona seemed to be requesting. “I ran out of whiskey. My kids snorted the last of the cocaine. I sold my last vials of hemlock and arsenic to a buddy who’s right now slipping them into his nagging ex-wife’s drinks. I fed my entire weed stash to a wild horse I just caught so he could mellow out before I put a saddle on him. And as for Special K, all I have is what’s in this box,” he ranted, unleashing years of pent up frustrations. He shook up the box of cereal with the name that meant Ketamine to those in the know, letting it all fall onto the floor. “Gee, no Ketamine left. Guess you and me will have to face the day without—”

“I need a fucking drink!” Leona screamed, pushing him aside and checking the cabinets herself for anything that would numb her pain, temporarily or permanently. "Or a toke. A snort. A fucking something!"

"I'm trying to help you," Stevenson offered, returning back to his kind self. According to Leona's best perceptions and intel, he had never experienced the buzz of firewater or the mind-altering perceptions of non-prescription pharmaceuticals.

"I can help myself!" she blasted back with clenched teeth while staring at the pain behind her eye, her hands blindly trashing whatever was in their reach. "I can fucking help myself!"

"So you said the first, second, and third time you were found behind the wheel, hammered out of your mind," Stevenson replied, grabbing hold of her wrists. He let them go once the fist above them loosened up. "According to my research on you, anyway."

Putting aside the issue of why and how a simpleton like Stevenson could have extracted that classified intel on her, she defended her position. "I was stoned, drunk, and tanked in my glory days. Never fucking hammered."

"What do you want?" Stevenson inquired, getting to the meat of the matter as he processed of cleaning up the mess of broken glass, scattered pictures, and previously filed papers from the floor. "What do you really want?"

"For people and life to stop fucking me around," Leona found herself saying and realizing. "And for the pain to all be over, which is… still very possible," she continued, bending down to the floor. Under a layer of broken glass lay a picture of Paul. It was one of the good ones, in which he and she were connected with regard to mind and spirit. Or so Leona thought they were anyway. "Paul, whoever he was or became is gone," she calmly declared, she somehow stopped a flood of tears running down her face after the second cold drop streamed down her shaking cheek.

"Yes, he is," he echoed. He was as kind a messenger for the truth as he could be.

"He could answer a lot of my questions and yours. And not just about this Casino situation or how to talk a big fish into taking the bait on a small hook," Leona mused.

"He probably could."

"Then maybe it's my sacred duty, honor, and pleasure to join him on the other side and…" Leona speculated, laying down the picture of her still beloved brother and picked up a piece of broken glass. She edged it over the old scars on her left wrist. *If I move the sharp edge closer to where the arteries are they would be severed cleanly and quickly, ending all of my troubles forever,* she pondered, for very real this time.

Stevenson's hand grabbed hold of Leona's right arm. "Do what you have to do, but please, help me clean up this mess first. Please?" he requested, calmly of course. As to what mess he was referring to, he directed

Leona's attention to something very specific, both with regard to task and location. "Over there, by the shower door and the clothing closet."

"Sure, why the fuck not," she conceded, preparing to give her last compliment while still alive. *My last deed on this planet, though it is a small one, maybe should be a good one*, she pondered. *It's the protocol to get into heaven, if indeed they can stand someone like me there or I can stand them as well. Just one good deed may outweigh all the bad ones or the ones that I thought were good that turned out bad.*

The last good deed before she took an exit from life stage left was something Leona could complete without screwing up by the looks of it anyway. Cleaning up Stevenson's trailer was easy and doable. Cleaning up the world outside of it was hard and impossible. In the end, such was futile. Boris would undoubtedly find any of escaped girls hiding out in the woods somewhere and re-enslave them. Or he would kill them and find other girls. Timolto would be replaced by another two-bit African dictator who would pay even higher money for weapons of limited or mass destruction. All of that would be in the holy cause of money, as it is money that makes the world go round, after all. And money was what Leona was paid so well in when she was Leon, one of the most effective mercenary any shithead US government-backed Corporate CEO could hire to eliminate his competition in strange and exotic lands.

"It's bad karma to leave this life with a fucking mess behind," she muttered as she sorted the savable clutter from the disposable trash in Stevenson's bachelor trailer. "If I don't clean up the messes that I can, I'll have to come back as a ghost, damned by something or someone to—" her mouth froze in mid-rant as her eyes spotted a picture of Stevenson she hardly expected in her worst nightmares or most speculative dreams. "This is you?" she asked after taking it all in.

"It is," Stevenson confirmed. He strolled over to her and glanced at the picture he'd apparently directed and intended her to see. "That's me with my wife."

"It wasn't Halloween or anything?" Leona asked of the woman next to Stevenson's wife whose face bore a striking resemblance to his. "Or maybe you lost a bet with the guys you play poker with at the cop shop, barber shop, or hardware store?"

"No," Stevenson said calmly, and introspectively, with a voice that went up an octave in pitch, maybe two. "That was me, then. Before I transitioned, he said with relief and pride."

Leona looked again at the picture of the woman next to Stevenson's wife and then back at Stevenson. They were indeed the same person.

"Who else knows?" she asked.

"Nobody here," Stevenson replied, regaining his

masculine baritone voice. “My new kids in my new family,” he continued, pointing to a picture of two young men at a skidoo party with happy smiles who were still enjoying the joys of being boys. “They still think I was born with a penis.”

“But they look like you,” Leona noted.

“They look like my brother,” Stevenson sighed. “Who got my second wife pregnant by artificial insemination. She wouldn’t let him do it the natural way, even though I said it was okay to date him and marry him after she and I split up and—”

“When were you going to tell me?” she interjected, rolling her eyebrows with distain.

Stevenson let the answer incubate in his head for a few intensely reflective seconds. Choosing the words with the utmost of care and discretion. “I was going to tell you about my having transitioned when we were both far away from here. Even if that where was in different places. As we both know, telling people you used to be a murderer, thief, embezzler, rapist, extortionist, or any other kind of ist is more socially acceptable than having lived as two different genders… or wanting to.”

Leona re-lived all of the truth of that reality yet again. She reflected on the ironies of it all; she also recalled how much of her valuable time on this planet she had wasted being Leon. The clock on Stevenson’s wall and the one outside of the trailer in the world ticked loudly. She refocused herself on what she could and should do with whatever time the Great Spirit still allowed her have on this planet.

"So, what do we do about Boris's operation, and the girls, and my snatched and probably dead parents? And everything and everyone else all of this is connected to?"

"What we can, righting one wrong at a time, I suppose," Stevenson offered, retreating back into his own head.

"This time you're answering a question with another question."

"And your fucking plan is to do what?" Stevenson pressed.

"For you to continue finding and using you're fucking inner power!" she shot back as a smiling, maternal lioness pleased as punch with the courage rediscovered by her lion cub, or more accurately, lion mate. "That's the first fucking time I heard fuck come out of your self-inhibited mouth. And you have no fucking problem with that!"

"Fucking right," he asserted.

"Who wrote the official report that Tom was drunk and Emily was stoned highway bypass after that high-speed chase with the State Troopers?" Leona asked, getting back to business.

“Most of the people I know or used to know anyway.”

“And who signed it?”

“Someone who I used to know all too well, if everything was done according to procedure, most probably, given her last promotion,” Stevenson postulated. “Sheriff McDermott now. Long ago, she was just Officer Karlata, who had the hots for me. And maybe loved me, too. Until I had to tell her it would never work out between us romantically unless she was very open minded.”

Those words open minded said it all to Leona. She packed up her bags and picked up the keys to Stevenson’s truck he had laid on the counter next to the stove. “There has to be something left at the scene of the accident after my father’s truck blew up.”

“Or someone who got out alive before it did,” Stevenson said. “We hope, anyway.”

“Or several someone’s maybe?” Leona added the third brain between them resurrected, activated, and firing on all circuits.

CHAPTER 18

The tire treads at the site of the fatal drive off the cliff overlooking the hundred-foot deep rapidly moving waters of the Dakota River were very real. They were indeed from Tom's truck. But there were two sets of tracks. One stopped three feet before the three-hundred foot drop off from which there was no return. The other clearly went over the side. Next to the former, were several sets of footprints revealing bearing military treads. The wreckage of Tom's truck was clearly at the bottom of the gorge. The mangled mush of metal was scattered among the rapids below. No one neither made nor born of flesh caught within that charred mash could have survived.

"So, this is where my father and his Sequoia accidentally ran off the road," Leona noted.

"Your father's what?" Stevenson inquired.

"Sequoia. The name he gave the truck he swore he would keep alive as long as he was," she continued, holding back the tears as best as she could. "Sequoia was a Cherokee Linguist who invented a written language his people could use to talk to each other in print. It impressed the hell out of the Palefaces, till Old Hickory decided to relocate his people to where he thought they would never be heard from again."

"I still know Indians who won't take or spend a

twenty-dollar bill because his face is on it."

"Apparently not the Indians in this town," she shot back.

"Money is something you get used to real quick when you got it. Then when you do get used to it—"

"Shhh!" Leona grunted at Stevenson as she heard something in the bush on the other side of the gorge. It was none other than her raven, recognizable by its voice as well as scar on its left leg. The messenger from the Beyond Realm, as Leona needed to believe anyway, flew out onto an exposed, precariously swaying branch of one of the pines burnt in the crash. The bird cawed again, looking toward Leona. Leona listened to what the raven was trying to convey to her say regarding the twisted metal and bits of what looked like flesh between them.

Meanwhile, still-in-the-real-world Stevenson examined the tracks of another vehicle, which had swerved a bit off the road but not enough to be demolished. "These tracks from a pursuit, or perhaps accompanying vehicle, they go south."

"Then we go north and track them down from there," Leona replied with 146 percent certainty.

"And you intuit this because…" Stevenson inquired.

Leona pointed to the black as coal raven. It motioned with its beak the exact northward course to follow. The bird then scraped the ground with its beak. Leona knelt down and smelled the dirt.

"Human tracks," she noted, regarding a set of footprints.

"Moose tracks," he noted.

"Or shoes that make them look like moose tracks," Leona replied, trusting her nose rather than her eyes.

"All forensic evidence says whoever was here went south."

"And my avian assistant, our assistant, says we go north," Leona countered. Sensing an ugly confrontation ahead, she came up with a putative solution. "You go south, following the evidence. I'll go north, following my gut."

"Which is maybe just your rumbling stomach because you haven't eaten anything and you're light headed now, and—"

"Trust me on this!" she interjected. "Please?"

"Fine," Stevenson conceded. "But be careful!" he commanded. "A woman out here alone, particularly one that looks as good as you and dressed so invitingly is very vulnerable to being—"

"Right. Being right." Leona asserted. "And able to take care of herself, even though others can probably take care of her better than she can." She blazed a trail into the woods, leaving Stevenson on the shoulder of the highway.

While Stevenson followed the tracks of the real

world cars and trucks, Leona kept moving forward on the paths tread upon by people, or ghosts, with moose shoes. Those tracks and the Raven kept pulling Leona farther and farther into the bush. They led to places where she herself had trouble walking. Her wounds from the shootout at the "very-much-not-okay coral" during the gun show had still not healed enough to allow her to run, but she tried running anyway. As predicted, she fell on her face twice and her ass three times. The final fall converted her into a one and a half-legged lioness determined more than ever to not come back before she had caught her prey.

Previous to that fall, and the tension-filled hushes of expletives voicing her discontent with them, Stevenson had been sending "U ok?" texts to check up on Leona. Three times she answered with a simple "Yes." The fourth time it was with a "Will be if U leave me alone." This fifth time, there was no text message to annoy her. Then when she checked to see what was going on with Stevenson, to ask him if he was okay, her phone registered no signal. It was an odd situation as there were no dead cell phone zones in the area that she knew about.

She pulled herself up out of the muck and pressed on in a Westerly direction, which the Raven, now joined by two avian buddies, seemed to be traversing. Twenty painful steps on the ground later, those two friends whisked away Leona's bird compass, out of her sight, and then range of hearing.

For reasons she couldn't determine nor control, Leona felt afraid in the woods for the first time in her life. Maybe it was because there was more bush to them than open. Or maybe it was because there was a mild buzz in the air, which was not the sound of silence. Or perhaps that woman inside of her had somehow shut down the male sense of where north, south, east and west was. She mused before when losing her sense of direction. But this time, it was not funny.

The sun disappeared behind thick, gray clouds, refusing to give her any clues as to where it was. In the ill-defined fog that moved in, she spotted leather tassels stained with blood on the branches of secondary growth bush then spots of blood on the ground. Those spots led to what looked like an ancient hiking trail that ended abruptly in a collection of thicker bush that surrounded her on all three sides.

Something on the other side of the thick brush moved. The sky became even darker. A set of innocent, terror-infused green eyes stared back at her from the bush. She froze. Whipping out her hunting knife, she approached the prey or predator in the bush with the shiny eyes. After three carefully taken and what she thought were soundless strides, an arrow whizzed by her. She ducked then heard screams coming from the bearer of those eyes.

A second arrow ended the life behind those ocular portholes with a decisive blow.

"Sorry about that," Leona heard from a bow-carrying hunter on the other side of the bush He approached the now dead prey, addressing it as a friend. "I had to do it," Tom continued, on bended knee. He was wearing the vintage; blood and mud-stained fringed buckskin coat he refused to retire. His left hand was wrapped up with a fresh, blood-stained bandage.

Upon closer examination, she saw the prey was something far more innocent than an escaped sex slave trying to hide out from her owners and find her way back home. "A coyote with a very human face," she said.

A traditionally eighteenth century-looking Tom removed a pair of twenty-first century examining gloves from his pocket then put them on his hands. He pulled his hunting knife from the sheath and proceeded to skin the animal.

"You had rabies, my friend. You nearly bit my hand off when I tried to offer you some of my jerky, after everything you and me have been through over the years," Tom said to the coyote with a tear running down his left cheek. "Your brains were mush. You weren't yourself. And what you have, or had, is contagious."

"Dad! I thought you were... ya know…"

"Dead?" Tom replied as he continued to skin the coyote he had put out of his misery. "If I convinced you, I probably convinced everybody else. Being dead sometimes helps you stay alive."

"Why?" Leona pressed.

"Because you can be alive somewhere else," he explained. "I'll explain it to you—"

"Later? When I'm older?" she shot back, quoting those words she was always told when her father didn't want to honestly answer a very real question. "Well, I'm older, smarter, and, on a good day, maybe wiser. I demand to know what went wrong."

"With my hand when I tried to make friends with this coyote, thinking he was my Spirit Messenger?" Tom replied.

"Something more this-side-of-the-rainbow than that. Such as why did the guns you said would backfire into the heads of the goons buying them at Boris's arms fair didn't? And why, when they did fire, they wounded and killed the people I was trying to save?"

"Orders," Tom explained, without a breath of hesitation. He kept his mind on skinning the coyote and his eyes away from Leona.

"Orders from Chief Boris?" Leona was terrified to ask but did. She pushed herself onto her good leg and used a tree to enable her to stand over the man who she hoped would prove wrong her worst suspicions.

"You're a smart girl, Leona. Smart enough to know… Hmmm," Tom said as he finished skinning the coyote. He looked up at her, his stomach grumbling with hunger loud enough for even her to hear it. "How do you disinfect a hide from a coyote with rabies?"

"You don't!" she insisted. "Rabies gets spread through the saliva."

"What about the meat?" Tom inquired as he carved off a large chunk of muscle from the animal's hind limb. "If you cook it well enough, is it safe? Boiling meat kills bacteria. It should kill viruses, too, right?"

Leona was in no mood to do a private biology lecture to a mature student. "Where's Mom?"

Tom directed his gaze back to the coyote, his words to his daughter. "Safe, protected, and sheltered," he said prophetically. "Safe, protected, and sheltered," he repeated to the dead coyote, in a whisper. He then turned to Leona and repeated that phrase two more times, begging her to understand the inner meaning and feeling within the carefully chosen words.

"Safe, protected, and sheltered from bastards like Boris or shithead traitors like you," Leona advanced, hoping the theory emerging behind her awakened eyes about Tom was wrong.

"It's like this, Leona," Tom said after a tense pause. He invited Leona to sit down in front of him for one of those crucial life talks. His tone bore a striking resemblance to the time he told her, when she was Leon, that there was no Santa Claus. It smelled like that other life talk when Tom explained to Leon that the sticky material coming out of his penis when he rubbed it was not urine, and that letting that sticky piss go into the wrong woman would lead him into a very wrong life. But this time the talk was political as well as person. "To beat the American Palefaces, we make deals with the Russian Palefaces. We can buy back America with Russian money. And we will. No more living on Whitey's welfare. No more getting hooked on his dope. No more having to send our kids to second rate high schools taught by old farts that hate us or young ones who think they give a shit about us."

Leona didn't give a crap about the politics of the speech, and Tom knew it. He continued anyway.

"If the Great White father in Washington won't give us back our land and rights to what's under it legally, we'll make some calls to our friends in Moscow. Or maybe we'll make friends with some other enemy country, to convince them that it's in their best interest to cooperate with us," he explained. Tom took in a deep breath then lifted up the skin of the virally-infected coyote with his knife. Maybe the coyote was infected with naturally occurring rabies or maybe it acquired a mind-altering, brain-killing disease from another one of Boris's germ warfare agents. Or maybe he had learned how to modify one of the toxins Leona had used to create neurological diseases in the lab so she could cure them. In any case, the coyote was out of its misery. Leona certainly wasn't, her condition of guilt, fear, and anger made worse by Tom continuing.

"Biological was used against us by American Palefaces for centuries. It's our chance to return the favor with the help of our Russian colleagues. We finally are in a position to sell them rugs, blankets, dream catchers, and 'Injun authentic' leather-fringed coats to the American Palefaces that have shit in them that's a lot more toxic than the smallpox that was in the blankets they gave to us. If the shitheads in Washington and Wall Street give us what we want, we'll maybe provide some revolutionary cures for those diseases that 'brilliant' First Nations scientists developed. Which of course we have had on hand all the time."

"There's something wrong in that entire plan, technically and ethically, ya know," Leona pointed out.

"No!" Tom blasted back, his emotions holding his reason hostage. "There's something right in it!"

"That got my brother killed. Your son."

Tom retreated back into himself. He tried to let himself be absorbed into the process and art of removing useful material from the slain coyote. "Paul should have stayed greedy," he said. "But he had to get spiritual. Then he turned ethical. Then stupid."

“Then dead,” Leona reminded her father, who perhaps was still inside of the deluded turncoat in front of her disbelieving eyes.

“I tried to keep him from getting killed,” Tom explained. “And I’ve been doing everything I could to keep you safe and alive.”

“Safe and alive are seldom the same thing,” she reminded Tom, hoping he would recall he was the one who had originally planted that seed of practical wisdom into her head. “But getting to matters more immediate… what does Boris know about me?”

“Nothing about your past and present anatomy, if that’s what you’re asking. My hand to God on that,” Tom replied, putting up his right arm up in a pledge to the Great Spirit he loved and the Christian Heavenly Father he probably feared.

“The God of money, greed, or cruelty?” Leona pressed.

“The God that rules all of us!” Tom blasted into Leona’s face.

“No, not anymore.” Leona got up and hobbled away, turning her back on the only old fart other than Granny she ever liked, respected, and loved.

“Where are you going, Leona?” Tom inquired, insisting the lesson and possibly the conversion continue. “Come back!” he pleaded as she felt the hard ground on her feet more painfully than ever. “You’re my only living son, I mean… daughter," he said, reaching out with as much love as he could. "I did all of this for you!" he finally blasted out from an angry place inside of him that was hurting him as much as Leona. "For you, our people, and your mother!"

"Who is safe, protected, and sheltered," Leona shot back, her back turned to him. "By shitheads I'll inactivate no matter what I have to do to them or you."

She turned around to Tom, facing him for the last time. He threw her his bow and two arrows. "Go ahead, finish me off," he screamed at her.

She seriously considered taking him up on his offer then hesitated.

"Go ahead and finish me off," Tom blasted out in a voice that felt possessed. Or perhaps it was Tom whose mind had been burned out by a naturally occurring or synthesized brain toxin. "Kill me in the service of your Visionary Mission," the demon inside of Tom continued, burrowing his tongue to deliver the words. "If you have the balls to. But, no, you don't any balls. You freak! Self-righteous bastard! Freak! Self-deluded witch, bitch, and…"

Tom ranted on. Leona turned around then calmly walked down the path out of the bush. He tried to follow her. She kept him at bay with the third digit on her right hand raised upward at him. He held his position, yet kept screaming at her. All the while she held her left thumb into her belt, enabling her to seem steadier, so Tom would not see how badly she was shaking inside.

CHAPTER 19

Leona somehow found Stevenson after emerging from the woods or maybe it was he who found her. They relocated to a rest area off the highway, parked close enough to get on the road quickly but far enough from it to not be spotted. The linear-sequential trained and conditioned lawman looked over the satchel filled with evidence he had been secretly collecting on Boris for the last year, trying to make some logical sense of it. Leona used a different methodology to figure out how to make right all that had gone wrong.

She looked out her rolled down window at the vastness of the Rez. She forced her tired eyes to be extra open, hoping something from the trees outside or the facts jumbling in her head would come together into a viable plan.

"Universal perspective," she remembered calling it when Rachel asked about the best way to find out a biological truth that was more than just another chunk of data. "Let the biological tissue or the data you got from it tell you what it needs to," Leona had said by way of further explanation. "Let Mother Nature reveal her secrets to you on her terms not yours," was the final word on the matter.

That way of problem solving was something Granny had taught her, and more often than not, it worked. The most important clue to what the Universe seemed to want Leona to figure out was centered on "safe, protected, and sheltered," the phrase Tom repeated several times to her. He seemed to want her to listen to it with an enhanced sense of desperation, particularly after she'd asked where her mother was, and her people were. Finally, the significance of those words connected to solution for the many problems at hand.

"I know where they are!" she proclaimed, startling Stevenson nearly out of his seat in the truck next to her. "I know where everyone is, and where we will…yes, yes!'

"We'll what?" Stevenson asked.

She opened the glove compartment and rummaged through the collection of donut coupons—still uneaten jelly glazed scones, toothpaste tubes, toothbrushes, and mismatched gloves then pulled out the collection of maps of the Rez and surrounding communities. They were the ones that had for years kept Stevenson from getting lost en-route to the routine calls to routine places to which he was expected know the directions.

"Safe, protected, and sheltered is here!" she said, pointing to a large blue area on one of the least chocolate-cream stained maps.

"Which is in the middle of a lake," Stevenson pointed out.

"According to this munios map," Leona asserted,

assuming Stevenson knew that munios meant white. Its literal translation was “those who have gone mad in the pursuit of money”, a condition which now seemed to infect lots of Indians as well. “It’s a Pitcarin Island thing.”

“Huh?” Stevenson replied.

“Pitcarin Island’s real location is different than all of the maps the English Navy had. And when the mutineers of the bounty accidentally found it, they knew they could hang out there for generations without being found by the prosecutors Captain Blye sent out to find them,” she explained. “Fletcher Christian’s kids and grandkids grew up on the island without ever being found by anyone: safe, protected, and sheltered.”

Stevenson still didn’t get it, but then again, he wasn’t supposed to. No one except Tom, his once very dedicated American Indian movement armed radicals, and the Elders who were most connected to the innermost spiritual secrets of their culture were supposed to know about the island that existed in the middle of a swamp. The un-mapped hideout that was un-seeable by air and under-reachable by land unless you knew the way in and out. Quicksand and rusty bear-traps on the shores of the island had swallowed up many Palefaces in pursuit of renegade redskins. Those that did make it through to solid and non-booby-trapped ground were shot from hidden vantage points above. Their bodies were then eaten by the wolves hawks and, according some anyway, Indians in need of sustenance so they could fight another day.

Leona explained the legendary history of "Safe, Protected, and Secure" after which Stevenson related the contemporary reality of the place. "It's a well protected backwoods fortress now, if it's the place I'm thinking of. The last time I asked about it, or accidently rode my horse past it, it's guarded by more than quicksand, bear traps, and sharpshooters with nineteenth century Winchesters."

"And you know this because? Leona asked.

"You have your secrets, and I have mine. Keeping some of them is the best way we can both stay alive, for each other."

"And still let Chief Boris build an empire of greed and cruelty using our sacred land as his capital?" Leona challenged.

"Patience is a virtue and a tactical necessity," Stevenson explained.

"Nothing ventured, nothing gained. And there is a lot to be gained by both of testing out a new weapon against Boris."

"An army of ravens to scare the shit out of him, to discredit him as a wimp who is afraid of birds?" Stevenson suggested. "Or a ray gun you can make materialize out of the center of Granny's medicine wheel by conjuring up Nicola Tesla's ghost?"

"I was thinking of something and someone we both have inside of us. Yes," she said after the foggy image had become focused into a crystal clear image. "A power of perception and action only transgender freaks such as us are allowed and privileged to access. RD," she delivered with a smiling face into his welcoming eyes.

"The worth of a warrior is measured by the Greatness of his and her enemies," he affirmed.

Leona could hear the third brain between her and "RD" saying "yes, you finally got it!" Stevenson picked up on his part of the plan, initiating it into action. He inserted his keys into the ignition then an assertive screech of the tires onto the highway for the first look-see at the enemy at hand.

To anyone who passed by and stopped long enough to look at it peripherally, Pitcarin Island west, aka "Safe, Protected, and Secure", had all the appearances of a fishing camp for eccentric, pampered rich hunters who wanted to play at being rustic: its appearance from the outside, anyway. Leona and Stevenson looked it over from the side of an old, officially out of service, logging road, which was now more washboard and crater than flat surface. The design of the cabins was still the same as when she recalled from the days when the family took vacations there, but there were many more of them now.

Most of them had bolt-locked windows, particularly the larger ones that seemed to be bunkhouses for no doubt involuntary inhabitants.

Civilian guards with regulation jar head military haircuts as well as longer haired goons she recognized from Boris's entourage patrolled around and between each of the buildings. They were all armed with weapons capable of emitting bullets, laser beams, and/or flames from their barrels. The perimeter was lined with electrical barbed wire and motion-sensing Tesla coils that could detect any unauthorized movement and spit out a bolt of manufactured lightening with deadly precision. One of those coils found a rabbit as it inadvertently hopped over the fence. It landed on ground, flash-roasted into a burning mesh of pulverized bones and charred flesh which was more ash than potential rabbit stew.

"So, why are they so afraid of rabbits?" Stevenson mused as they perused the rest of the complex.

"Granny said this was sacred ground that belonged to the Great Spirit which, if disturbed, would cause it to stop protecting the two legged creatures on top of it," Leona commented.

"And what are they protecting?" he continued.

"Right now I'm more concerned with who they're protecting from us or anyone else from the outside world," Leona said, as the sites of her high-powered binoculars happened upon a building with an open window. That view revealed a woman inside wearing an electric Chief Boris brand shock collar. She was a relatively plain looking niece, who seemed too old and used up to be very sellable. But she was exceptionally well guarded.

"Your mother?" Stevenson asked, reading Leona and noting the especially worried expression on her face.

"Wearing a collar like the rest of the girls," Leona replied as she got a closer look at her prematurely old, homophobic mother, looking across a small brook. A closer look with the binoculars revealed Emily was looking with fear and worry at a larger building. That structure was more basement than house, its windows replaced by bars. On the other side of the bars she spotted Amanda 4 and Yolanda 2, along with the other young women who'd tried to escape their masters at the arms fare. It was a special punishment house by the tortured looks on their battered faces. Adjoining it was a new prefab house with slits for windows. A cattle truck pulled in, unloading its cargo into it. The pieces of fresh female meat walked into it slowly, their ankles hobbled with chains.

The girls were fresh, confused, and naked. Those who were slow to move quickened their pace as soon as their collars were zapped. They walked even faster when guards jovially shot bullets at their feet. A limo drove in.

The driver stopping the car and let Boris out to inspect the goods. He approved of the new shipment then waved them on to their new country cottage, promising them all the pleasures of any mansion if they behaved themselves. He carried himself off more like Santa Claus at a Christmas celebration than Joe Stalin at his favorite Goulag as he threw out packages of new designer clothing to them, each of which had their new slave name printed on it.

"Do they look beaten or helpless?" Stevenson asked. "If we give them the weapons from our now shared arsenal will they use them?"

"I don't know," she replied, handing over the binoculars to Stevenson. "But there's one thing I do know. Besides the fact that there's more than just human cargo here." She referred Stevenson to another wing of the compound. Tucks came in with metallic weaponry on one end. Cars left leaving with happy customers at the other. "By the looks of it, Boris's bargain basement is back in full unofficial business with a lot of the people you're in official business with." She then referred Stevenson to the new leader of the security squad, none other than Officer Karlata McDermott.

"Selling people as slaves is reprehensible. Destroying a human life is unforgivable. Arming dangerous people with more guns is deplorable. But at least they're not selling bio-weapons here, which if they are, would cause big time harm world-wide, irreversibly on a mass scale," Stevenson noted, putting issues of what in front of who, for the moment. "Unless he got a hold of…"

He turned abruptly silent, his open jaw frozen in place.

Leona grabbed hold of the binoculars and took a look for herself. "So, Boris did get hold of my notes," she said, noting another semi-underground building opening up for business. It was a biological laboratory by the looks of the lab-coated nerds milling in and around it. A junior member of that team was dragged out of it in a blood-stained lab coat, an electric collar around her neck. She was promised a death worse than any experimental rats by the goons if she put up any more resistance on her way to the holiday cottage or if she said anything to her new roommates there.

"Rachel!" she gasped. "How and why did she come out here? I never told her where I was!"

"Maybe Chief Boris did," Stevenson proposed.

Never did Leona need Carlos's services more than now. Perhaps the self-taught, self-made inventor of anything that needed to be invented could come up with a machine that would neutralize the electronic surveillance equipment and the weapons carried by the Indian and paleface goons. Maybe Carlos's laser gun could be set to a frequency where it detected and shocked anyone bearing the asshole gene, a chromosomal abnormality, which Leona was sure existed. But Carlos was not here. It was the only good news of the day, for Carlos anyway.

She recalled that Carlos and Granny claimed life never gave a problem without a solution. As for that solution, now, this very day, it would require her and Stevenson diving deep into themselves and using all of the resources at their disposal. She opened up her eyes very wide. The final draft of an idea came through, one that was so off the charts it had to work.

CHAPTER 20

Stevenson gathered all of the firearms at his disposal while Leona drew up the battle plan on a large piece of paper, which he was reviewing. The command center for the two-person Commando team was a room at the Cactus Flower Hotel. The Flower was establishment on the White Trash side of town where the more money you paid the clerk, the less questions he asked of the guests and their intentions.

He sat down on a mattress of the bed, which contained more used needles and condoms than foam. Leona remained in the bathroom a bit longer than he was comfortable with.

"You okay in there, Leona?" he barked out, concerned not only with how she was doing but by his need to empty his bladder. He knocked for the fifth time then decided to work on the doorknob. It was not locked. He entered then lost all concern for his own bodily functions as saw Leona as she never appeared to him before.

"Leon?" he gasped, gazing at Leona in her new presentation. Such boldly featured Redneck macho jeans complete with a Rodeo Belt over her shapely hips and legs. A beard was attached to the soft skin on her hairless face. Around that face lay blackish-brown hair with no strand more than two inches long, chopped up with equal imprecision on both sides.

“Well, what do you think?” she asked as Leon.

“Well, look at you,” Stevenson replied in a high pitched female voice he hadn’t used for years, impressed with the transformation that made Leona look almost exactly like Leon back in the good ole boy days.

“Well, look at you too,” Leona commented, equally impressed with the believability of Stevenson’s transformation. The only hair on his body was now a brownish-blonde wig on top of his head, except for the narrow slits, which were his newly shaped eyebrows. Over his artificial C-cup breasts lay a beige hiking sweater. Around his waist was a sort of matching skirt. All was book-ended on his nail-polished feet by open-toed stiletto heels designed for being looked at rather than for walking.

They looked at each other in the mirror, each next to the other. Leona asked the critical question. “So, can we pass as a couple of urban hikers out for a stroll in the woods who got lost?”

“I hope so,” Stevenson said, taking note of Leona’s chopped hair.

“Relax,” she assured him. “It’s a wig. Just like yours. I would have cut off all my hair to a buzz cut except for a promise I made to someone a long time ago to never cut my hair off.”

“To who?” he asked.

"My father," she replied, oscillating between anger and grief. "The man he used to be, anyway."

The plan was simple and complicated. The first few stages of it went off without complication at the outer perimeter of Boris's compound. Jason carted a large duffle-bag around his shoulders in the lead. Regina, aka RJ, shuffled behind in her heels, pulling a wheeled carrier containing in two large suitcases. "You could have left those clothes that you think make you prettier than you are behind in the van on the side of the highway. Whoever steals them will look better in them than you ever did," Jason barked back to Regina as they came within hearing range of three guards at the outer perimeter of the compound. Jason laughed when his wife Regina nearly slipped into the muck again in her fashion footwear.

"And you carting along all that moonshine," Regina whined regarding the heavy load on her hubby's shoulders. "You say you have a bad back and can't do any lifting at home, but you sure as shit won't go anywhere without your precious home grown 'medicine' you get drunk on every night and when you get behind the wheel."

Before the guards could inform them they were trespassing on private property, Regina escalated the argument with her hubby, scolding him for letting their van break down and forcing them to hike off the road to look for someone who could offer automotive assistance. Jason told Regina to go back to the van, but Regina insisted on coming along to be sure moonshine-toting, bubba-bellied “Daniel Boone Jason” didn’t fuck up anything else. Regina then laced into Jason for thinking he could blaze a trail to their final destination in Bismarck without a map, accusing him of intentionally getting lost as well as stranded so that she and he would miss her sister’s wedding.

The argument was convincing to Karlata McDermott, a senior enforcer by her uniform and the way she wore it. It was amusing to the guards under her command. It was hysterical to the goons in the compound as Jason walked closer into the middle of it, providing colorfully degrading insults directed at Regina’s character and gender.

The kvetch parade continued, entertaining more of Boris’s very male goons en route. With each colorful dig at womanhood put out by Jason and every display of frustration by Regina, the guards seemed distracted, which allowed Leona and Stevenson past the front of the luxury cabin housing where Emily was being maintained. Jason’s large jug of homemade moonshine tasted mighty fine to the palate of whatever yahoo decided to try it. Everyone bearing a penis decided it was worth a swig.

The argument ended with Jason asking the guards for

gas and a wrench, insisting he could and would go back to the van and get it going himself. Regina vented her marital grievances to any of the guards who would listen and some of them who didn't. They were one-way conversations, which ended with each of the guards being thankful they weren't married themselves. Meanwhile, the wife-cursing woman discretely dropped explosive devices at key places between the buildings and at key points in the electronic surveillance and voltage delivery systems. Jason allowed himself to be seen by no one except for Emily.

"Leon?" Emily whispered from behind the window she was allowed to have opened from the kitchen she was allowed to cook in. By the looks of it, Emily was allowed such privileges as long as she kept her dog collar on and kept the guards with the remote zapping devises happy in the palate.

From the other side of the window, Leon shushed Emily, sneaking her a key to liberate herself, along with a set of instructions scribbled on an ad for discount electrolysis. Emily crossed herself with thanks to the Lord then acknowledged her gratitude to her finally-returned son with a large brownie and recently-cooked buffalo-burger sausages.

"Your favorite," she smiled at Leona. "For my returned son who —"

Leona shushed Emily even harder as she felt herself

noticed by Karlata McDermott, the only sober enforcer or guard in sight. The fact she was still breathing indicated McDermott was still convinced she was Jason, a trespasser who, after the entertainment and moonshine was done with, would be shot dead and fed to the slave girls as stew, if they obeyed their masters of course.

To divert McDermott's attention, Leona put on her best sloshed-on-imaginary-beer-Jason act out.

Meanwhile, Regina threw out witty digs aimed at Jason's stumbling, barfing, and belching. All the while he flirtatiously complimented the goons on their anatomy and offering the best of hers. As Regina, Bill became the center of attention and interest, and such postponed McDermott's elimination of Jason.

Hmm... Bill Stevenson's a far better cunt tease than I ever was, Leona thought as she drunk-stumbled into the vicinity of the holiday house. She sloshed by the windows holding Yolanda 2, Amanda 4 and now Rachel, dropping off newly made-master-collar releasing keys to them, along with instructions in Latin, in which ex-Catholic now Pagan-Buddhist Rachel was still very fluent.

Jason, forgetting the gas can and wrench Karlata authorized him to take, stumbled off into the woods, working on his third beer. En route he bellowed out his favorite drinking song, Beethoven's *Ode to Joy* sung in German. The signal for everything to happen was the third stanza. The lyrics for that stanza were given to the girls in the bungalow. Leona hoped Emily would understand the written instructions for the plan and prayed none of their guards would.

Regina, disgusted with her husband Jason, refused to join him in the bush. She insisted that someone from the "fishing camp" go back into the woods to fetch him, promising whoever did anything he wanted from her. It was a great amusement that lasted for three minutes and was long enough for Leona to set up whatever guns she and Stevenson had carried into the compound under the guise of being mind altering moonshine and body-flattering clothing.

She inactivated the machismo guard assigned to retrieve his drunken ass from the woods with a single kick to the sternum then set up several of the automatic firearms and explosives from her still-un-inspected backpack amidst the brush, with timers and strings connecting them that would fire several of them at one time. She retained the most powerful firearms for herself. By the time Jason got to the third drunken stanza of the tune, Leona counted down the signal.

The Apocalypse arrived on schedule. Bullets from Beethoven's ghosts in the woods showered the compound, pinning the unsuspecting guards to the ground. They all were astounded at how anyone could have gotten past the perimeter. They were also startled as why the moonshine that tasted so good to the tongue was doing so many not-so-good things to the shaking muscles in their legs and arms.

Having not ingested in the brew, Karlata McDermott organized whoever could still stand against the unseen intruders. She ordered the men under her to shoot dead anything in the woods that moved. Several of those shots grazed Leona. None broke any bones or blew up any vital blood vessels, not yet anyway. Even if they did, she had to keep going and avoid falling into Karlata's sights if she was to continue what she started.

Meanwhile, Karlata radioed what had happened in to headquarters. By the time she'd dialed the number, she was punched into unconsciousness by the most helpless woman in camp.

"That's for what you did to Tom," Emily grunted. It was the first time she'd used her fist, rather than her tongue, to take out another human being. The once-pacifist-hippie, now God fearing homophobic Christian, grabbed Officer Karlata's gun, aiming it at her head. "And this is for what you did to Paul."

En route to liberating the girls in the holiday house, Leona pushed herself between her mother and a half-conscious Karlata. "Leona. How do I pull the trigger on this thing?" Emily asked.

"You don't," she replied, thankful for being addressed by her mother with her female name. She took the gun from Emily and shot a round smartly into Officer Karlata's left foot then another into her right arm. The blood splattered back into Emily's terrified face. "I'm the necessary evil, Mom, not you," she explained as another one of the home-made explosives she planted on the compound blew up not twenty feet behind her.

"And liberator?" Emily said, pointing Leona's attention to the cattle truck being driven by Stevenson, who didn't look very much like Regina anymore. All of the girls in the compound were being ushered into the back of it by Rachel, Yolanda 2, and Amanda 4. Those three girls, along with two others, were armed with weapons they had stolen from their captors after they had somehow taken back their dignity.

"We gotta go," Stevenson yelled to Leona. "Now!"

She heard something at the other end of the compound countering that request. Trucks emerged from the woods behind the ten new bombs she had set up went off. Some took out the buildings and people they were intended to. Most didn't.

"Go, get them out of here!" she commanded Stevenson. "While you still can."

"Leona!" Emily screamed from the back of the escape vehicle, reaching out to grab hold of her re-found daughter and son.

While spraying machine gun fire at the oncoming

trucks, Leona pushed Emily back into the truck. She closed the door, knocked on the hood, then motioned for Stevenson get the hell out, immediately.

The rest of the day became black as night. Leona and Leon merged into one entity, which was both lion and lioness. That composite of male and female energy took out every other predator in the jungle. Somehow, the lone beast was winning, but not on its own. Someone behind her had come into the game, shooting from behind the trees at everything and anyone with the capability of killing her. Every piece of machinery advancing her way blew up. Every pursuer on two feet fell to the ground or used said appendages to run into the woods with battle cries.

"I didn't sign up for five hundred bucks a day for this bullshit."

The assailants and deserters all fled, as did the mystical helper from the beyond realm. Stevenson and the girls were worlds away by now. Leona heard nothing but the quiet. The silence was broken by the voice of someone she had written off as dead or worse.

"So, how many of them did we neutralize? How many minions of evil did we eliminate?" Tom asked, a smoking gun in his hand and several other weapons of individual destruction strapped around his shoulder.

"Enough of them, I hope, for now," Leona replied. She felt satisfied and relieved until she turned around again and saw a face that made her think otherwise. “Except one,” she said, noting the face of her second rescuer. She quickly drew her gun on Boris, aiming it at his head.

“I am impressed,” Boris boasted. He took a swig from a flask of vodka just like the good old days in that Iraqi village when he and Leon were the only survivors of massacre in which both sides were decimated. “I am impressed with all of you,” he went on. “You, Tom, for standing up for yourself. You, Leon for finally standing up to me. And you, Leona, who I still hope is in there. And who I will gladly accept as a lover.”

Leona looked at Tom, who now had his gun aimed at Boris as well. “Please, both of you, do what you want to do. All of this is short term gain for you which will cost you long term profits,” Boris continued. He laughed at the guns pointing at him, as well as those holding them. He strolled around the bodies littering the battlefield. He collected money, jewelry, and body parts from the dead and dying like it was an Easter egg hunt. “This operation here… I got what I wanted from it. And who I wanted.”

Leona noted that Boris’s actions and tone threw Tom off his game, whatever it was. That diversion was long enough for Boris to whip out his pistol and shoot Tom in the chest, the former AIM activist who claimed the eyes behind his head were always wide open fell to the ground. She rushed to his aid then was stopped from doing so by another bullet from Boris's pistol; it put a paralytic hold into her shooting hand. Then she felt and saw Boris's boot heel pushing her other hand into the blood-soaked dirt.

"Cowboys always beat the Indians," Boris informed Tom, who by some miracle or intention, was still breathing very painfully. "You should have known that." He then turned to Leona. "And you, my Leona. Who I suspected was Leon for… well, longer than you thought I did. What do you have to say about all of this?"

Tom replied with mumbled words in his Native tongue, emerging from his mouth in a flood of blood and angry volcanic defiance.

"What did he say?" Boris asked Leona.

"It's a good day to die," Leona translated as she saw in slow motion her father pull out his traditional hunting knife then throw it squarely into Boris's back. The indestructible Russian who had never even been grazed in the line of fire fell onto the sacred First Nations ground he had so sadistically desecrated. His legs shook like dried fall leaves in a brisk winter wind.

Leona rushed over to Tom, ensuring he was all right. They were the usual lies that you told a dying man who didn't want to die. But Tom was ready.

"No," he said as he took in his last breaths, which became rattles. "It is a good day for me to die. And a good day for you to live."

That having been shared, Tom breathed his last with a satisfied smile on his face. Such left Leona with an uncertain one on hers, particularly with regard to Boris.

"Kill me," Boris begged. Finally, he was experiencing the pain of dying and the confusion that came with it. "It's the honorable thing to do, and God help your pathetic, morally-obedient soul, it's the only thing you can do."

"But I can't kill you," Leona smiled at him, lovingly, while stroking his cheeks. "You saved my life, let's see, five times, and I only saved yours four times. I owe you." She went into medic mode and stripped off patches of Leon's clothing for bandages to stop the bleeding in Boris's open wounds so his legs could experience the full agony of spastic paralysis. "I must save your life, so you can spend the rest of it wearing, let's see…" she pondered. She retrieved from her pocket a special item she stole a few days earlier from Boris's special collection of goods. "This!" she exclaimed, showing Boris an electric slave collar upon which she engraved his name with an appropriate number. "Zero, zero, zero."

"So you have become a necessary evil," Boris said proudly. "What would you say if I said I was proud of you for finally growing a set of balls along with those breasts?"

"I don't give a shit about what you say to me or

think of me, not anymore," she spat back. Pulling herself back on her aching and wounded legs, she pulled Boris around by the dog collar. She dragged him into one of the only vehicles still operating in the Pitcarin Fishing Camp. "When we get back to town, you will tell everything about what you've done and who you've done it with to the people on my side of the morality line"

"And if I don't consent to—" Boris protested, his arrogant last rant stopped by Leona buzzing a remote control in her pocket. It sent a jolt of pain down his paralyzed spine.

Leona didn't laugh when Boris was unable to do anything about what she was doing to him. Instead, she reviewed many lessons about what the world was and what it could be. She planned rather than merely dreamed how she and Stevenson, as the woman and man they were to the core, could both fix and transform the world. Yes, it was a good day to live!

The End

Author Bio:

Kristin Kennedy served with distinction in the US Army as a soldier and special ops mercenary in forty-eight (48) countries.

During her transitioning from being male to female, she does spiritual work for people of many faiths. She is with, a national outreach organization. Today she is a writer of transgender fiction.

Other books published by Wicked Publishing

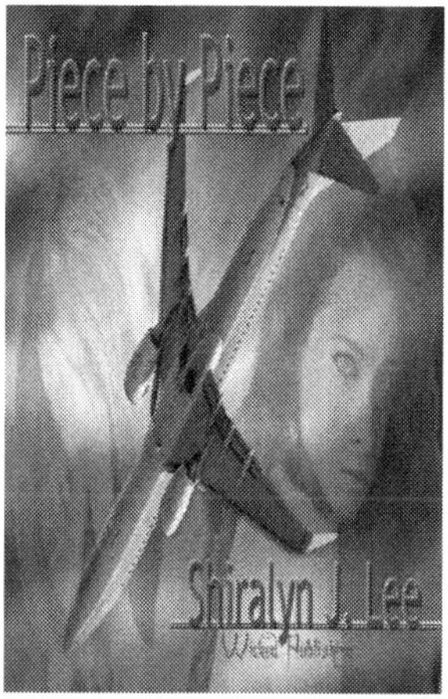
Piece by Piece
Shiralyn J. Lee

Ronni Meyrick
Hero

OCEAN
Shattering
Rainbows
Wicked Publishing

Clicking Stones
NANCY
Tyler
GLENN
Wicked Publishing

To submit your manuscript to Wicked Publishing:

Submit the completed manuscript electronically. Please include the following: A one-page plot summary including a working title, the genre, and the word count. Complete author biography, and synopsis for the back of the book. Include author information: Name, mailing address, and email address. Include any previous publications, including free to public forums on the internet. Advise us if the manuscript was published previously. If so, let us know the status of the manuscript with the previous publisher.

General Editing Requirements Page set-up: House edit rules supersede all others. These include the use of serial commas and all thoughts and emphasized words are in italics. Font is to be in Times New Roman. Font size: 12pt. Please do not add a space between paragraphs! 1.5-line spacing. There must only be one space between sentences. Do Not use the tab to indent your paragraphs. All scene breaks must have some sort of symbol to separate the scenes. Clearly indicate chapters, and the manuscript must have already been submitted and corrected by Beta Readers.

67344857R00157

Made in the USA
Charleston, SC
10 February 2017